"So you prefer richer brother?

With that, Jerome closed the door firmly behind him.

Megan immediately marched angrily after him and burst into his study. "Now, you listen to me, Mr. Towers," she stormed. "I—"

Suddenly she was pulled against his hard body, her mouth captured and parted as he bent his head to kiss her. Finally he murmured huskily, "I knew my accusation would get you in here."

Megan pushed hard against him. "You obnoxious, overbearing—"

"I could hardly kiss you out there in the hallway," he explained. "Anyone could have seen us."

"You didn't have to kiss me at all!" she snapped, still breathless from the touch of those warm lips on hers.

"But I did," he said calmly. "And I intend to do so...often."

CAROLE MORTIMER

is also the author of these

Harlequin Presents

294—THE PASSIONATE WINTER
323—TEMPTED BY DESIRE
340—SAVAGE INTERLUDE
352—THE TEMPESTUOUS FLAME
365—DECEIT OF A PAGAN
377—FEAR OF LOVE
383—YESTERDAY'S SCARS
388—ENGAGED TO JARROD STONE
406—BRAND OF POSSESSION
418—THE FLAME OF DESIRE
423—LIVING TOGETHER
430—DEVIL LOVER
437—ICE IN HIS VEINS
443—FIRST LOVE, LAST LOVE
452—SATAN'S MASTER
473—FREEDOM TO LOVE

Many of these titles are available at your local bookseller.

For a free catalogue listing all available Harlequin Romances and Harlequin Presents, send your name and address to:

HARLEQUIN READER SERVICE
1440 South Priest Drive, Tempe, AZ 85281
Canadian address: Stratford, Ontario N5A 6W2

CAROLE MORTIMER

point of no return

Harlequin Books

TORONTO • LONDON • LOS ANGELES • AMSTERDAM
SYDNEY • HAMBURG • PARIS • STOCKHOLM • ATHENS • TOKYO

For
John and Matthew

Harlequin Presents edition published January 1982
ISBN 0-373-10479-0

Original hardcover edition published in 1981
by Mills & Boon Limited

CHAPTER ONE

'IT's no good, Megan, I have to go.'

Megan tucked the bedclothes more firmly about her mother. 'You aren't going anywhere, not with a cold like that.'

'But I have to,' her mother insisted nasally. 'We need the money, you know that.'

Oh yes, she knew they needed the money. She had heard of nothing but how badly they needed money since her return yesterday. But she would not sell her share of the farm, not for any amount Jerome Towers cared to offer. This farm could be made to work for them if they tried hard enough, and now that she had been dismissed from the hospital she could help her brother Brian with some of the work. Finch Farm wouldn't even be noticed in the amount of land the Towers estate already had, but to them it meant a livelihood. At least it would, when they could make it work.

'They won't miss you up at the house for one morning,' she told her mother firmly. 'Besides, we wouldn't want the new owner to catch your cold from you, now would we? With all that wheeling and dealing he does each day he needs all his strength.'

'He doesn't wheel and deal, dear,' Emily Finch collapsed back on the pillows, her face pale. 'He's a business man.'

'And he makes a huge profit doing it, which means someone else suffers for his gain. Look how much his lawyer offered us for this place—peanuts!' Megan dismissed disgustedly. 'And all the time you're working in

5

his house as a kitchenmaid!'

'It isn't as bad as it sounds, Megan. The housekeeper, Mrs Reece, is a very nice woman, and as for Freda, the cook . . . .!' She gave a husky laugh, unwittingly increasing the irritation in her throat and sending her into a spasm of coughing. 'Oh dear,' she sighed, 'I really don't feel very well.'

'Of course you don't, Megan said impatiently. 'Now you just lie there and I'll get you a nice cup of tea.'

'But what about my work at The Towers?' her mother frowned worriedly.

'What about it? Let someone else peel the man's potatoes for lunch,' said Megan almost angrily.

'There isn't anyone else—and he doesn't eat potatoes.' Her mother gave a wan smile.

'Trying not to get a middle-aged paunch, I suppose,' Megan muttered on her way out of the bedroom.

'What did you say, dear?' her mother called after her.

She appeared back at the bedroom doorway. 'Nothing of importance. Now just try and get some rest.'

Her mother frowned. 'But what about Brian's breakfast? And feeding the hens? And then there's Bertha to see to.'

'Bertha?' Megan cut in with a laugh. 'I'd forgotten we still have old Bertha.'

'Of course we have,' her mother said indignantly. 'She's in the nature of a family pet.'

'A cow, a family pet?' Megan teased.

'She isn't just any cow, Megan. She was the first one we were able to buy when we moved here ten years ago. When your father died last year we sold the rest of the herd—we had to—but I refused to part with Bertha. She's more like a friend.'

Megan shook her head. 'I never thought of you as a sentimentalist, Mum.' But she was secretly glad that

Bertha was still with them, she was a favourite with her too, although she wasn't going to admit it.

'I'm not a sentimentalist,' her mother said sharply. 'I've never had to be, with the burden of this farm around our necks. But that cow is just something special.'

'Okay, Mum,' Megan grinned. 'I'll see to Bertha and the hens, and then I'll cook Brian's breakfast.'

'And The Towers?' her mother still persisted.

Megan frowned. 'You aren't expecting me to do that too?'

'Well, if you don't I shall have to get up and do it. If I don't work I don't get paid. And at the moment, with you out of work, we need that money badly.'

She knew her mother's words weren't intended as a rebuke, nevertheless she knew she had put an added burden on her mother and brother. Until she had left the hospital she had sent money home every month, but now that she was out of a job things were going to be even more strained monetarily.

'All right, Mum,' she sighed, 'I'll do that too.'

Her mother's worried frown disappeared. 'Oh, thank you, love! I usually start at ten o'clock.'

'Yes, Mum. But it's only eight o'clock at the moment. Don't worry, I won't let you down and be late. I have plenty of time to do all those little jobs you consider essential before going to The Towers.'

'I should get Brian's breakfast first,' her mother advised sleepily. 'He'll be in in a minute.'

Megan yawned. 'What time did he leave?'

'Five-thirty, as usual.'

'My God!' she groaned. 'And I thought getting up at seven o'clock at the hospital was bad enough. How does he do it?' The thought of getting out of bed at that unearthly hour horrified her.

'Because he has to.' Her mother lay back with her eyes closed. 'He works much too hard for a boy of twenty-two.'

Megan had noticed last night how tired her brother was looking—and no wonder, if he was getting up at that time of morning. 'Does he need to do so much?'

'Well, there's no one else to do it. We're just starting to get back on our feet, just starting to make the land pay for itself. It wasn't easy to turn from a livestock farm to growing vegetables, but as you know, we couldn't afford to restock.' They heard the back door slam. 'That will be Brian now.'

'Then I'd better get a move on. I'll bring your cup of tea to you in a minute.'

Brian still looked tired. Three years older than herself, he bore the worry of the farm without complaint. He was no more eager to sell his share of the farm than Megan was, but their mother was all for getting rid of it.

Their father had died of an incurable disease the year before, and during the last months of his life he had run up many debts because of his inability to do the necessary work about the farm. Brian had managed as best he could, but in the end they had been forced to sell the livestock to pay the debts. Megan had just started her nursing training at the local hospital twelve miles away at the time, and her mother had insisted she carry on with her career. And now she had been thrown out through no fault of her own!

'Hello, Sis.' Brian sat down wearily. 'Where's Mum?'

'She isn't feeling well this morning, so she's having a lie down.'

His brown eyes, so like their mother's, looked worried. In fact he was very like their mother to look at, stocky and short like her, with her brown hair and eyes. Megan took after their father, her long fair hair almost silver, her eyes green splashes of colour in her thin pale face.

'It isn't anything serious, is it?' He took the mug of tea she held out to him.

'Just a cold.' Megan put a slice of toast on the tray with her mother's tea. 'But I don't think she should neglect it. I'll just take this in to her and then I'll cook your breakfast.'

'Don't rush on my account,' he said morosely. 'I can't do much, the damned tractor's broken down again.'

Megan took the tray through to her mother, coming back to put Brian's bacon and eggs on to cook. 'Any idea what's wrong with it?' she referred to the tractor.

'No. You know mechanics aren't my line. I rang The Towers and asked Jeff to come over and have a look at it.'

'Jeff?'

'The new manager.'

Megan frowned. 'I didn't know they had one. What happened to Ralph Coates?'

'Jerome Towers sacked him. But Jeff's a nice bloke, and he knows a lot about mechanics.'

'I suppose he has to,' she grimaced, sitting opposite him as he tucked hungrily into his breakfast. 'Jerome Towers only knows how to sit behind a desk all day and make money.'

'What have you got against the man?' he chuckled. 'I know he made an offer for the farm, but that's no reason to hate his guts. Jeff says he's a really great bloke, very fair.'

'Well, Jeff would say that.' She sipped her coffee, which was all the breakfast she ever had. The thought of eating the type of breakfast Brian was enjoying made her feel heartily sick. She had never been able to face food this early in the morning. 'He's his employer. And I would hardly call the offer he made for this farm fair.'

'But it was, Megan, very fair. He was offering well over its real value.'

'Why?'

He frowned. 'What do you mean, why?'

'Why was he offering more?' she asked suspiciously. 'Does he know something we don't?'

'Like what?' Brian laughed.

'Well . . . like maybe someone else is buying this land up for development, and he wants to buy it cheap and sell for an astronomical price. Or maybe he——'

Brian shook his head, still smiling. 'You watch too much television, young lady. Mr Towers wants to buy this farm and land because it's right in the middle of his estate. Dad bought this land off the old Squire when he was selling off plots to give him money to run the rest of the estate. Mr Towers has managed to buy most of the other smallholdings back, and he would like this one to complete it.'

'We aren't selling!' Megan said stubbornly. 'Just because he has pots of money he thinks he can buy anything. Well, this is our home, and we're staying put.'

'Are you sure you want to after that trouble at the hospital? Rumours are bound to start when people realise you're back, and it won't take long for the truth to filter back from Redford.'

Colour flooded her cheeks. 'It wasn't my fault, and you know it!'

'Of course *I* know it. But other people are going to believe the evidence, Megan. It didn't just happen once, it happened twice, and as far as a lot of people are concerned, especially in this close-knit community, that's just once too many.'

'I've already explained to you, Brian, the time on the

ward he just pulled me into his room and wouldn't let me out—and he actually broke into my room at the nursing home.'

'There wasn't any forced entry.'

'I was down in the kitchen making myself a cup of coffee, and when I got back—well, he was there waiting for me.' Megan blushed at the memory of it.

'You could have screamed for help,' Brian pointed out reasonably.

'I was just about to. But he'd always seemed so nice until then, always polite and friendly, and I thought I could reason with him.'

'Even after the attack he made on you on the ward?' her brother derided.

'I managed to get free that time, and he hadn't made a move like that since.'

'I don't suppose he needed to, not when one of the doctors had seen you lying on the bed with him, the front of your uniform unbuttoned.'

'He was in a fever and had the strength of ten men. Dr Freeman and Sister Miles believed me when I explained what had happened,' Megan defended.

'Until he was found in your bedroom at midnight. Didn't either of you realise the night staff would miss him from his room? A hospital isn't like a hotel, you know, not even if you are a private patient. You can't just go in and out as you please.'

'I do know, Brian,' she said indignantly. 'And I told you, he wasn't there at my invitation.'

'Oh, I believe you. But I doubt many other people will around here. You'll be the scandal of the neighbourhood.'

'As long as you and Mum believe me I don't care about anyone else.'

'You will. Village life can be very uncomfortable if

you're the subject of the gossip,' he warned seriously.

'They may not find out about it, there's always that chance. I don't intend telling anyone, and he'll go back to London. He wouldn't even have been in Redford if he hadn't been visiting someone in the area when he was taken ill.'

'Appendicitis, wasn't it?'

'Mm,' she grimaced. 'But he was a private patient. And sometimes he acted like it.'

'I thought you said he was friendly and nice.'

'He was, most of the time, but that didn't stop him being aware of the fact that he was paying for his treatment.'

Brian stood up. 'Well, I hope for your sake that none of this filters back. And don't forget Jeff will be over later to look at the tractor.'

'Before ten, I hope.' She cleared the table. 'I have to take over for Mum at The Towers,' she explained. 'I wouldn't want Jeff to come to the house while I'm out and disturb Mum.'

'I don't suppose he'll be too late, he has his own work to do. The tractor's out in the yard, I managed to get it back this far. Tell Jeff it keeps cutting out, something to do with the flow of petrol, I think. I'll be up in the top field if he needs me.'

'What about the keys?' she called out as he reached the door.

'In the lock.' He smiled. 'I doubt anyone would want to steal it.'

Megan mentally agreed with him as she stood at the sink washing the dishes. The tractor could be clearly seen from the kitchen window, and like the rest of the farm was badly in need of attention. Its red paint was badly rusted, showing its age. Megan had noticed yesterday that the farmhouse was badly in need of a coat of paint, the white paint having gone grey and was flaking in places.

It was curiously relaxing feeding the chickens. They were such uncomplicated creatures, pecking away at their feed all day, occasionally at each other, seemingly in fun, laying a few eggs if they felt like it, and then sleeping in their nice warm roost at night. What a life! And what Megan wouldn't give for their simple happiness.

Now she just had to see to Bertha, make sure her mother was comfortable and had everything she needed, and then she could get over to The Towers. The trouble was actually finding Bertha. She looked everywhere for her, in the shed, in the neighbouring fields, but Bertha wasn't to be found.

And then she saw her! She was being led back into the dusty dry yard by the man Megan presumed to be Jeff from The Towers. He was very handsome, extremely so, and she was made to feel conscious of her grubby denims and tee-shirt. Then she dismissed the feeling of inadequacy, no one could look bandbox-fresh working on a farm, and Jeff would appreciate that fact.

The only trouble was, this man managed to look reasonably smart, the beige corduroys and black sweat-shirt he wore emphasising the muscled perfection of his body. He was tall, almost six and a half feet she would have said, at least ten years her senior, with thick black hair brushed back from his face, a strong tanned face with a deep cleft in the chin. She couldn't see what colour his eyes were from this distance, but she would take a bet on them being blue. They had to be, in every other respect this man was her ideal, his eyes had to be blue to complete that ideal.

She stood and watched him as he led the cow over to where she stood, the docile Bertha looking perfectly happy to be taking this morning stroll. The man at her side moved with the grace of a cat, lightfooted and very sure, making Bertha look more ungainly than usual.

Megan was wrong, his eyes weren't blue, they were brown, a deep velvety brown that on reflection she thought she preferred. But they didn't look very friendly at the moment, appearing to look down disdainfully at both her and poor Bertha. And Brian had said he was a 'nice bloke'! Still, maybe he was when you got to know him. After all, by the look of things Bertha had been wandering again. Megan couldn't remember a time when she hadn't done it, but maybe being a newcomer to the district Jeff hadn't heard of Bertha's wanderlust.

'The absent Megan, I presume,' he drawled, his voice husky, with no trace of an East Anglian accent, pointing to him not being a local of Norfolk. Megan wondered what had made him decide to work in an area that was flat and lacking in outward beauty, although she had always thought it had a certain charm of its own.

'Yes—I mean, no. What I really mean,' she blushed at her confusion, 'is that yes, I'm Megan, and no, I'm not absent any longer.'

He frowned. 'I thought you were training to be a nurse?'

'I was,' again she blushed, 'but I—I've been ill. They thought I wasn't strong enough to carry on such arduous work,' she invented, her fingers crossed behind her back as she told the lie.

'They?' He raised one dark eyebrow.

'Er—yes, they. The senior nursing officials.'

'I see.' He was watching her closely with narrowed brown eyes. 'And are you back to stay?'

'Oh yes,' she smiled. 'I'm going to help Brian on the farm.'

'And won't that prove rather—arduous too?' he

queried mockingly.

Megan gave him a sharp glance. Surely he hadn't heard of her dismissal and the reason for it? No, he couldn't have done. It had only happened two days ago, hardly time for her to have realised it herself. Her one consolation in the whole affair had been the fact that they had asked Roddy Meyers to leave the hospital too. Of course he was recovered from his illness, but it had still afforded her some satisfaction to know she hadn't taken the blame alone.

'Oh, I'll only do the light jobs to start with.' That one little lie was taking her deeper and deeper into a web of deception. She just hoped Brian wasn't friendly enough with the man to tell him the truth. 'And the fresh air will do me good,' she added for good measure.

'Yes, you are a little pale.'

She was naturally pale, but she wasn't going to tell him that. She blushed at the intentness of his arrogant gaze, feeling as if he stripped the clothes from her back and explored every curve of her body. It was extraordinary to feel this way with a total stranger—even if he was so attractive.

'I see you brought Bertha back,' she patted the cow affectionately on the neck. 'Where did she go this time? Not the Towers?'

He nodded. 'I'm afraid so.'

'Well, well, Bertha, you can't be as old as we thought you were.' The Towers was at least a mile away, and much too far for the aged cow to have walked, she would have thought. 'I hope she didn't trample on the snooty Mr Towers' flowerbeds or anything?'

Was it her imagination or did he seem to stiffen? 'I beg your pardon?' he said in a stilted voice.

'Sorry,' Megan blushed, 'I shouldn't have spoken like that about your employer.' She gave an involuntary jerk as their hands touched as she took Bertha's rope out of his grasp and tied the cow to a post. This man had nice hands, long and hard, and very confident. It was the hand of a man who wasn't afraid of hard work, and seemed to go with the rest of his rugged appearance. 'But don't you find him snooty?' she asked interestedly.

'I can't say that I have. Did someone say that he was?'

She shrugged. 'It was just the impression I got. Still, it isn't important. The tractor is over there,' she pointed to the stationary vehicle.

'Yes?' He appeared puzzled.

'The tractor Brian called you about this morning.' Surely this man couldn't have these looks and body, and be a fool? That just wouldn't be fair. But he didn't look a fool, far from it. There was a shrewd hardness to his eyes, a determination to the firm mouth and jaw. No, this man looked far from being a fool. There had to be some misunderstanding. She frowned. 'Didn't you take the message yourself?'

'I couldn't have done,' he told her abruptly, 'or I would have known what you're talking about.'

She tried to ignore the sharpness of his tone. He had had to walk back here with Bertha, and knowing the speed the cow walked it must have taken him ages, so she could make excuses for his shortness of temper. 'Brian called The Towers this morning and asked if you could look at our tractor. I was under the impression that you had agreed to come over.'

'I see. Well, perhaps you could put—Bertha?—into a shed, and I'll take a look at it.' He began striding towards the tractor. 'Any idea what the trouble is?' he shot the question over his shoulder.

Megan came back from settling the cow into her stall. 'Something to do with the fuel getting through,' she told him vaguely, no more familiar with the workings of this machine than Brian was. She knew nothing about mechanics; she had tried to learn how to drive once, but much to the relief of her driving-instructor she had given up after a couple of lessons. She had turned out to be one of those people whose personality changed as soon as they got behind the wheel, becoming aggressive and unmanageable.

'Thanks,' he taunted her lack of knowledge, 'that will be a great help.' He lifted up the side covering of the engine before getting up behind the wheel and attempting to start it. The engine gave a couple of stutters, roared into life, and then stopped. 'Fuel starvation,' he muttered as he came back to look inside it.

'Do you have any idea why?' asked Megan.

'Not yet,' he derided. 'The fuel not getting through can be due to any number of things.'

'Oh.' So he really did know a lot about engines. She watched him as he worked, offering him her handkerchief when he got oil on his hands.

'No thanks,' he refused the snowy white square. 'I can quite easily clean up when I get back.' He put up a hand to his brow, wiping away the fine film of perspiration that had appeared in the heat of the day.

'Now look what you've done!' Megan exclaimed. 'You have oil all over your face,' she explained at his querying look.

He moved to stand just in front of her. 'Wipe it off,' he ordered huskily.

Although made as a request it took the form of a challenge, the nearness of him, the utterly male earthy smell of him making her tremble. He looked down at her from his great height, seeming to know of her reaction to him, to the unhidden warmth of his brown eyes. She stared fixedly at his mouth. He had such a nice mouth, the lower lip fuller than the top, pointing to a latent sensuality. She had never met a man like him before, challenging and infinitely male.

'Well?' His gaze on her mouth was almost like a caress.

Megan had heard of men like him, men with the charisma to captivate and hold at a glance. And she was very much afraid she had been more than captivated. 'Yes?' she asked breathlessly, unable to look away from the magnetism of his face.

'The oil,' he reminded her with amusement.

'Oh—oh yes,' she blushed at her stupidity. 'Could you bend down a little? You're so tall I can't reach,' she explained.

'Certainly.' His head bent and he put his mouth against hers, holding her with just the touch of his lips, like a trapped butterfly. He made no effort to touch her in any other way, their bodies only inches apart, but still not touching.

When he finally stepped back Megan stood like one in a trance. She had been kissed before, plenty of times, but not like that, never like that. It had taken her breath away, her strength, her very will. That he was a master at the gentle art of seduction she had no doubt. And he knew exactly what he had done to her—his teasing brown eyes told her so.

'Well, Megan,' he said softly, his breath stirring her hair, 'it appears that you now have oil on your face too.'

'I do?' she breathed, completely mesmerised.

'You do.' He took the handkerchief out of her hand and gently wiped her cheek. 'Have dinner with me tonight?' he asked huskily.

'I—I beg your pardon?'

'Have dinner with me,' he repeated, smoothing back

her hair from her face.

'I—I can't,' she refused reluctantly. She wanted to go out with him, very much, but she could hardly leave her mother on her own when she wasn't well.

He straightened, his hands falling away from her hair, those beautiful brown eyes narrowing. 'Boy-friend?'

She blinked her bewilderment. 'Boy——? Oh no,' she smiled. 'My mother, actually.'

'Your mother?' He raised dark eyebrows. 'Aren't you old enough to choose for yourself who you go out with?'

Megan laughed. 'Of course I am. That wasn't what I meant. My mother isn't feeling well. Just a cold, I think——'

'In your expert opinion,' he cut in mockingly.

She flushed. 'A year's training hardly qualifies me for anything.' Unwittingly her bitterness showed. She had been a good nurse, had enjoyed her work and it had all been taken away from her by Roddy Meyers. If she ever met him again . . .! But that wasn't likely to happen, he had already left the hospital on his way home before Megan herself had left. 'But I think I can diagnose a cold,' she added dryly.

'How about later in the week?'

'Well, I—I don't know,' she said reluctantly. 'I'll be working up at The Towers this week and——'

'*You* will?' he frowned darkly.

'Mm. Mum works in the kitchen, you see. And—well, we need the money. So if I'm working up at the house perhaps we could have lunch together one day. I think Mum usually finishes about one.'

He seemed to withdraw from her, moving to shut the hood of the tractor. 'Maybe we could,' he agreed non-committally. 'I think your brother will have to get someone out to look at this. I can't pinpoint the trouble.

He can borrow one of The Towers' tractors until this one is on the go again.' He turned to leave.

Megan watched him go, a frown on her face. 'Jeff?' she called after him, watching as he slowly turned, his hair appearing almost black in the strong sunlight. 'I can call you Jeff, can't I?' she asked uncertainly.

He shrugged. 'Why not?'

Why not, indeed? From his suddenly cold manner she must have done something to upset him. But what? 'I wasn't refusing to go out with you,' she said hastily. 'It's just that it's a bit awkward this week.'

He nodded. 'Next week, perhaps.'

'Or lunch . . .' she trailed off as he strode away without turning.

What on earth was the matter with the man? He couldn't just walk out of her life like this, not when he had suddenly become so important to her. And yet he was walking away, was even now turning the corner at the end of their dirt driveway. He'd gone!

And she would have to go too if she was to get to The Towers in time for work. They could have walked down together if he hadn't disappeared so quickly. Oh well, perhaps he was just the moody type. She just hoped he was in a more friendly mood the next time she saw him.

She took her mother another cup of tea before leaving, assuring her that all the jobs around the farm had been taken care of.

'No one told me how good-looking Jeff is.' She plumped her mother's pillows for her.

Her mother frowned. 'Jeff Robbins?'

'Mm. He's really gorgeous!'

'If you like that type. Has he just been down, then?'

'Mm. He says the tractor needs expert attention. And tell Brian he said he could have one of The Towers' tractors. Although what Snooty Mr Towers will say to that I don't know.'

Her mother gave her a disapproving look. 'I hope you didn't talk about him like that to Jeff. He's very loyal to Mr Towers.'

'Mm,' Megan sighed. 'He didn't seem to like it when I made a comment about his employer.'

'What sort of comment?' her mother asked worriedly. 'You didn't say anything insulting, did you, Megan? Jeff's a friend of Brian's, and——'

'Don't worry so, Mum,' she soothed. 'Whatever I said it didn't seem to bother him. He asked me out to dinner a little while later.'

'Jeff did? But I thought he was taking out Rachel Saunders.'

That wouldn't surprise her; he looked the sort of man who would already have a girl-friend, and Rachel Saunders was very beautiful. She and Megan had been at school together, although the two of them had never been friends, as Rachel was three years her senior. Megan remembered she had had a crush on Trevor Dunn, the boy Rachel had become engaged to. The engagement had later been broken, but the dislike had stuck.

'Well, I'm not going, so it doesn't really matter. Now I'm off to The Towers. Don't forget to tell Brian about the tractor.'

'I won't, dear. And tell Mrs Reece I'll try and be in tomorrow.'

'I'll tell her no such thing,' Megan said firmly. 'You're going to stay right here until you're completely better. I don't mind going to The Towers.' Especially if she got the chance of seeing Jeff Robbins again.

The Towers was a grey stone building, a massive place with at least fifteen bedrooms. It had belonged to Henry

Towers until his death last year, and now it belonged to his nephew Jerome. Old Squire Towers, as Henry had been called, had run into debt over the estate, refusing to ask his nephew for help, claiming he was a pompous snob who would gloat over his uncle's misfortune, and instead the Squire had resorted to selling off parts of the estate.

Of course the nephew had bought back all these small-holdings—except theirs!—and so old Squire Towers might just as well have asked him for the help in the first place. But at least this way he had been spared the humiliation of approaching his nephew with a begging bowl. The fact that Jerome Towers was a millionaire, and his uncle was scraping together every penny he could, should have told the former that unless he offered his help it would never be asked for. Obviously by the sale of the land he had never offered.

Megan walked up the long gravel driveway, admiring the rambling beauty of the house and accompanying stables, and walked around the back of the house to knock nervously on the kitchen door. It wouldn't do for her to knock on the front door, not when she was just hired help!

A short, plump, red-faced woman opened the door, her ample frame covered by a paisley patterned overall. This just had to be Freda, the cook.

'Yes, love?' she smiled.

Megan smiled back shyly, and explained about her mother's illness and the fact that she had come as her replacement.

Freda was suitably sympathetic about Emily Finch's illness, although she looked rather harassed. 'Thank goodness you're here, love, that's all I can say,' she sighed. 'Patsy's not come in today either, and I've just cooked Mr Towers' brother's breakfast and there's no one to take it up but me. I don't like showing myself in the main part of the house. I'm a cook,' she smiled happily, her three chins wobbling, 'and a cook's place is in the kitchen.'

And if this woman was any advert for the success of her own cooking it must indeed be first class!

'Isn't it a bit late for breakfast?' Megan asked, hanging her jacket up behind the door. She had changed into a tan wool blouse and deep brown skirt, as her denims were hardly suitable for working here. Especially if she had to run all over the house with breakfast trays!

'That it is. But he's been having a bit of a rest. He only arrived yesterday.'

'Well, so had she, but that didn't mean she could laze about in bed all morning. In fact, she had been up earlier this morning than she usually was. 'I didn't know Mr Towers had a brother,' she said interestedly, having thought him an only child.

'Neither did we.' Freda put a rack of toast on the tray with the plate of sausages, eggs and tomatoes. 'Not until he arrived.'

He sounded exactly like his brother, thoughtless and selfish. 'Shall I take the tray through now?' Megan offered.

'I'll just put this pot of tea on, he likes tea in the morning. There!' she looked down at her handiwork, 'that ought to keep body and soul together until lunchtime.'

As it was almost that now, Megan wouldn't be at all surprised. 'Which way is the dining-room?' she asked,

'Oh, he isn't in the dining-room, love,' Freda smiled. 'He's upstairs in his bedroom.'

'Oh,' After her recent experience at the hospital she wasn't sure she dared risk going to any man's bedroom.

'At the top of the stairs, fourth door on the right,'

Freda directed, not noticing her reluctance. 'It's very good of you to stand in for your mum, Megan. A good worker, is your mum.'

Megan knew that. Her mother had never been able to sit idle while there was work waiting to be done, and as there was usually plenty of work to do on the farm . . . 'The rest will do her good,' she smiled. 'And I'll do my best to take her place.'

'I'm sure you will, love. I didn't mean——'

'I know you didn't,' Megan laughed, knowing very well that this friendly lady had meant it as a compliment to her mother. 'I'll try not to be long with this,' she promised.

She had the impression of unobtrusive luxury as she walked through the house, The Towers having been completely redecorated and refurnished before the new owner had moved in. The workmen had been working on the place for weeks before Jerome Towers moved in. Megan didn't pause over her admiration of the new colour schemes, not wanting to arrive at the bedroom with a cold breakfast.

Not that she didn't think the man deserved it. It was typical of Jerome Towers' brother to arrive on the doorstep unannounced and then want to be waited on hand and foot. Breakfast in bed at ten-thirty in the morning, indeed! Brian had already put in five hours' work by this time! It just didn't seem fair.

She knocked on the wood-panelled door, hearing the mumble of some sort of answer. She knocked again, just in case it had been an instruction to wait and not to come in.

She heard another mumble inside, a crash as something hit the floor, and then the door swung open.

'You!' she exclaimed in horror, the tray almost falling out of her hands.

Standing in front of her, his blond hair tousled from sleep, his eyes bleary, his only garment a pair of blue silk pyjama trousers resting low down on his hips, the beginning of his recent appendectomy in evidence, was Roddy Meyers!

CHAPTER TWO

THE sleepy look left his eyes and he leant casually back against the doorjamb. 'Well, well, well,' he drawled mockingly, 'if it isn't Little Megan Finch!'

She had recovered from some of the shock by now— but not all of it! And she had thought she would never see him again, had *hoped* she would never see him again. 'What are you doing here?' she demanded accusingly. She must have the wrong bedroom, must have turned left instead of right, but that still didn't explain this man being here.

The last time she had seen him had been when he had been pulled off her as she lay helpless on her bed, helpless because he had just pushed her there before attempting to make love to her. They had been discovered by a senior nursing officer as she did her rounds of the nurses' home, and although Megan had claimed her innocence her story hadn't been believed, because this man, Roddy Meyers, had claimed she had invited him there, had said she had been attracted to him from the first. Then of course the first incident in his private room had been brought up.

She couldn't blame the people in charge for thinking the worst, not on the evidence they had. But she would never forgive this man for the lies he had told about her. He was despicable, and she hated him more than she had ever hated anyone in her life.

She pushed past him to put the laden tray down on the dressing-table. Damn Jerome Towers' brother, he would have to wait for his breakfast, be it cold or not. She had something much more serious to deal with at the moment.

'I asked you a question.' She turned on Roddy Meyers, her green eyes sparkling angrily. 'What are you doing at The Towers?'

'I would have thought it was obvious,' he taunted, obviously not realising how close he was to being struck. 'I'm staying here.'

'What is this?' she snapped. 'A hotel?'

He raised blond eyebrows. 'Not as far as I know. What do you mean?'

Megan sighed, wondering why it was that she had resisted this young man's advances so relentlessly that he had had to resort to force. He was good-looking in a youthful sort of way, twenty-five years of age, blond hair that was worn much too long, blue eyes, a handsome face, and yet she just hadn't been attracted to him. That he hadn't felt the same indifference had been obvious from the first moment they met; he had asked her every chance he got if she would go out with him. That her constant refusals had been responsible for her downfall she had no doubt.

'I mean that Jerome Towers seems to have more guests here than the staff can cope with,' she said rudely.

Roddy frowned. 'Rome does?'

'Rome?'

'I've always called him that,' he dismissed.

'Bully for you,' she taunted.

'You don't like him?' he guessed shrewdly.

'I've never met him,' she didn't directly answer the question. 'Just why are you staying here?'

'Have you forgotten, I was politely requested to leave the hospital?' His sarcasm was unmistakable.

'Well, at least it was politely done. I was *thrown* out,' she remembered vehemently.

'Mm, it was a shame about that, but——'

'A shame!' she echoed shrilly. 'It was more than that to me. You've ruined my career, you know. I'll never get another job in a hospital. I'll never know how you knew which room was mine, I certainly never told it to you.'

He grinned. 'I asked your friend Tracy.'

Megan's eyes widened in amazement. 'And she told you, just like that?' She had always thought Tracy her best friend at the hospital, had even promised to keep in touch, and now it turned out that Tracy had helped this man get her sacked. Somehow that didn't sound like Tracy.

Roddy sat down on the bed, pushing his long hair back from his face. 'Not just like that, no. I told her you'd invited me to your room, that you were expecting me, and that I'd forgotten your room number.'

'And she believed you?' Megan groaned. She knew a lot of the other girls sneaked boys into their room, although this was expressly forbidden in the hospital rules, but she had never been fond enough of anyone to take the risk of getting caught.

He shrugged. 'She had no reason not to. I tell a very convincing story.'

'Oh, I know that!' to her cost!

'Mm,' he grinned. 'What a coincidence us both being in the same area.'

'I happen to live here,' she snapped.

'At least now I know I won't be bored.'

Megan glared at him. 'Don't count on me to alleviate your boredom.' She picked up the tray again. The food would be cold now, she would have to go down for a fresh lot.

Roddy was watching her. 'Where are you going with that?'

'To get fresh food and then take it to its rightful owner.'

'Leave it,' he ordered.

'I——'

'It's my breakfast, Megan,' he said patiently.

'But Jerome Towers' brother——'

'Me,' he nodded.

She nearly dropped the tray for the second time. '*You* are his brother?' She just couldn't be that unlucky.

'That's right,' he smiled at her horror. 'Half-brother actually, but that's never counted for much.'

Just her luck! If anyone should ever find out that he was the man involved in her dismissal, and that he was staying so close to her home, they would never believe her innocence. 'Does he know why you were asked to leave?' she asked almost reluctantly.

Roddy laughed, taking the tray out of her hands and pouring himself a cup of tea. 'He doesn't even know I was asked to leave,' he informed her calmly, 'let alone why.'

'He doesn't?' She almost sighed her relief. Maybe if Roddy Meyers was no more eager than she was to have their past meeting made public knowledge they could keep the scandal to themselves.

'No,' he bit into a piece of buttered toast, 'I just told him I'd been discharged.'

'And he believed you?'

'He had no reason not to. So now you're working for

my brother?' He eyed her speculatively.

'No, I'm not, I'm just helping out. And now I know you're here I don't intend helping out any longer,' she told him angrily. 'I'm leaving, and right now!'

He moved in front of the doorway to stop her exit, his hands on her upper arms. 'Don't be like that, Megan. You've been against me from the first—why don't you like me?'

She wished she knew that herself. 'Maybe you try too hard,' she evaded. 'Whatever the reason, I want you to take your hands off me.'

'Oh, come on, Megan, I still want to go out with you,' he said coaxingly. 'And now there's no patient/nurse relationship to stop us we can——'

'I don't remember that stopping you before!'

'No, well——' he smiled, 'you're beautiful, very desirable. You can't blame a man for being persistent.'

'*That* persistent I can,' she said indignantly. 'I should hate you for what you did to me.'

'But you don't,' he murmured softly, his gaze fixed on her parted lips. 'Oh, Megan, I——'

'Roddy, are you going to get up to——' the voice trailed off as the man came to stand in the open doorway, his brown-eyed gaze levelled on them as they stood close together.

Megan wrenched away from Roddy Meyers' embrace to face Jeff Robbins, and the censure in those deep brown eyes made her squirm with embarrassment. She had wanted to see him again, had intended making sure she did, but not when she was in Roddy Meyers' arms.

'I see yu're already awake, Roddy,' Jeff Robbins drawled, his gaze flickering over Megan almost insolently before passing back to Roddy. 'And being entertained too, by the look of things.'

The younger man grinned. 'I was just getting to

know the new maid.'

'I am not the new maid!' Megan denied vehemently.

'No, she isn't,' Jeff Robbins agreed. 'Miss Finch is deputising for her mother,' he explained abruptly.

'I was just trying to persuade Megan to go out for a drive with me this afternoon,' Roddy lied, knowing he had her trapped.

'Really?' Again brown eyes raked over her. 'And did you manage to persuade her?'

'She's a bit hard to pin down to anything definite,' Roddy grinned. 'But I live in hope.'

'Don't we all?' Jeff drawled.

All humour left Roddy's face. 'Have you been after her too?' he queried resentfully.

'No one has been "after" me!' Megan cut in on their conversation, wishing Roddy Meyers would shut up, and that she could persuade Jeff Robbins that this situation wasn't like it looked. But he didn't look any more ready to believe her than they had at the hospital two days ago.

'Haven't they?' Jeff asked, eyes narrowed.

'No! I——'

'Hey, Rome, I think she's embarrassed,' Roddy mused.

Rome? This was Jerome Towers? But it couldn't be— could it? But what other explanation could there be for him to be walking about the house? The estate manager would have no need to do that. Why hadn't he told her this morning who he was? No wonder he hadn't known about the tractor he was supposed to mend!

Why hadn't he corrected her mistake? Had he enjoyed listening to her make a fool of herself? The reason he had changed his mind about taking her out became obvious; he would hardly want to date someone who was working as kitchen help in his own house.

Everything the old Squire had ever said about this man suddenly seemed true—he *was* a pompous snob.

He was still watching her with narrowed eyes, obviously knowing of her surprise. 'Maybe you should get some clothes on, then she wouldn't feel that way.'

'Megan's used to seeing men without their clothes on,' his brother dismissed.

Jerome Towers' contempt seemed to increase. 'Is she now?' he grated.

'Of course she is—she's a nurse, isn't she?'

'How do you know that? Did you know Megan before today?' Jerome queried suspiciously.

'She was on my ward, weren't you, love?' Roddy looked at her for confirmation.

Megan blushed, the look in her eyes willing him not to reveal any more about their previous meeting. 'Yes,' she nodded, her gaze still on Roddy.

'Before she was ill, of course?' Jerome Towers enquired coolly. 'If she had you for a patient, Roddy, I can quite understand her not being strong enough to carry on,' he added mockingly.

Roddy looked at Megan with amusement. 'I didn't realise. . . . I wondered why you suddenly disappeared,' he taunted.

Megan gave him a resentful glare. 'Well, now you know,' she snapped.

'Yes,' he grinned, 'now I know.'

'Shouldn't you be getting back to the kitchen, Miss Finch?' Jerome Towers asked harshly. 'I'm sure Freda could do with your help.'

Colour flooded her cheeks at his intended rebuke. 'Yes, of course. If you'll excuse me.'

'Gladly,' he drawled.

'Megan?' Roddy Meyers stopped her at the door. 'Can I take it that our drive is on for this afternoon?'

Her eyes flashed. 'You——'

'Maybe then you could tell me about your illness,' he added mockingly.

Megan gave Jerome Towers a sharp look, biting her lip as she read the contempt in his gaze. What gave him the right to be so high and mighty? 'Yes, all right,' she agreed to Roddy's blackmail—for that surely was what it was. But she would tell him a few home truths this afternoon! 'What time?' She couldn't look at either of them in her anger, but stared down at her hands.

'About two-thirty?'

'Okay. I'll meet you downstairs.' She didn't want her mother and Brian getting to know of the meeting, especially Brian. If he found out their connection he was likely to seek the younger man out and challenge him to a fight. Then there would be no possibility of hiding the past.

'I'll pick you up at your home,' he insisted.

'No! No,' she said less sharply, knowing that Roddy could be deliberately troublemaking if he knew how much she wanted to keep him away from her home. 'I'll enjoy the walk over.'

'All right,' he shrugged. 'She knows her own mind,' he told his brother laughingly.

Jerome Towers' expression remained grim. 'So I've noticed.'

Megan shot him a resentful glare before leaving the room, running down the wide flight of stairs as if the devil himself were after her. Seconds later she felt as if he were!

'Miss Finch!' Jerome Towers stood at her side as she reached the bottom step.

It took all her courage to turn and face him, to face the disapproval that she knew would be in his face. Why should he be so disapproving? He was the one who had lied and deceived her. She felt an absolute fool now when she thought of the way she had acted with him, the things she had said. And she had let him kiss her! No!—she had let *Jeff Robbins* kiss her, not this arrogant stranger.

'Yes, Mr Towers?' she asked in a stilted voice, looking steadily into those censorious brown eyes.

'Freda said you took Roddy's breakfast up fifteen minutes ago,' he said curtly.

Whatever she had been expecting him to say it hadn't been this. She frowned her puzzlement. 'Yes?'

'If you are to continue deputising for your mother until she is well enough to return I would advise you not to spend too much time in my brother's bedroom, no matter what your relationship may have been with him before you came here.'

Megan gasped. 'What has Roddy been saying?'

'He's hardly had time to say anything,' Jerome Towers said dryly. 'But your own response points to my assumption being a correct one. And the other staff will draw their own conclusions if you take fifteen minutes to deliver his breakfast every morning.'

'Why, you——'

'I'm only telling you this for your own good,' he interrupted her angry outburst. 'It's up to you whether or not you take my advice.' He walked past her, turning when he reached what she assumed to be his study, or office, door. 'And, Miss Finch,' he paused when he had her attention, 'I think I can take having a date turned down without the girl having to resort to her mother's illness as an excuse. You had only to say you had something going with Roddy. Unless of course you were trying to decide whether the richer brother might be a better bet.' He went into the room and closed the door firmly behind him.

Megan didn't give herself time to think, marching angrily across the marble tiled hallway and bursting into what turned out to be a study. 'Now you just listen to me, Mr Towers!' she stormed at the man standing just inside the room. Almost as if he had expected her . . . 'I——'

Her words were cut off in mid-flow as she was pulled against the rigidness of a male body, her mouth captured and parted as Jerome Towers bent his head and kissed her.

'Oh!' she gasped as he released her, still held in the firm grip of his hands.

He looked down at her. 'I knew that would get you in here.'

Her eyes were wide. 'Is that why you . . .?'

'Mm,' he nodded, his warm gaze on her parted lips.

Megan pushed hard against him, struggling to be free. 'You obnoxious, overbearing——'

He let her go, moving to sit in the leather chair behind the desk. 'I could hardly kiss you out there in the hall-way. Anyone could have come along and seen us.'

'You didn't have to kiss me at all!' she snapped, still breathless from the touch of those firm lips on hers.

'But I did,' he said calmly. 'Now, what *is* your relationship to Roddy?'

'I'm not telling you!' her eyes flamed with feeling. 'And just in case you haven't heard about it, the Squire no longer gets the first night of love with the local maidens!'

He raised dark eyebrows. 'Are you a maiden?'

'Mind your own damned business!' She slammed out of the room, the sound of his mocking laughter follow-ing her.

Freda was busy preparing lunch when Megan entered the kitchen a few minutes later, so she took over the peeling of the potatoes.

'Are you all right?' the cook asked. 'You're looking a bit flushed,' she explained her query.

'I'm fine,' Megan mumbled.

'Young Roddy hasn't been making passes at you, has he?' Freda tutted. 'He is a lad!' She shook her head, a smile on her lips.

'Is he in the habit of making passes?' Megan couldn't help her curiosity.

'Well, he made a couple of advances towards Patsy when he stayed here last. In fact, I wouldn't be at all surprised if that isn't the reason she's off sick today—you know how her Donald can be. Roddy wouldn't leave the poor girl alone, that's why I wondered if he'd——'

'Nothing I can't handle,' Megan cut in briskly, wondering what Freda would say if she knew she was in more danger from Jerome Towers than from his young brother.

'That's all right, then.' Freda was obviously relieved. 'Would you get some mint in from the herb garden out the back?' she asked, the makings of pastry in her mixing bowl. 'I do like my potatoes to have a bit of mint in them.'

'But I thought Mr Towers didn't eat potatoes.' Megan blushed at Freda's questioning look. 'Just someting Mum said,' she mumbled.

Freda nodded understanding. 'Mr Towers doesn't bother with much food at all. I'm always telling him he doesn't eat enough, but he says he doesn't see the point of over-indulging.'

Megan wondered if he had the same attitude to all life's appetites. From the way he had kissed her, twice, she didn't think he did. His mouth against hers had been frankly sensual, pointing to an experience that hadn't been gained by abstinence.

But he had no right to kiss her whenever he felt like it, as if it were his due or something. If he ever tried to kiss her again she would—she would—She sighed; she would kiss him right back, she knew she would. Much as she tried to keep up her prejudiced dislike of him, the truth of the matter was that on acquaintance she found him all too disturbing for comfort.

'Maybe he's afraid of middle-aged spread,' she made the same bitchy comment to Freda that she had made to her mother only that morning, although now she knew it to be untrue. Jerome Towers wasn't thin, not unpleasantly so, his shoulders wide and powerful, tapering down to a slim waist and forceful thighs, his stomach flat and firmly muscled. No, he was a man at the peak of physical fitness, and the closeness of his lithe body against hers had had an arousing effect.

'At thirty-two?' Freda scoffed. 'Go on with you!'

Megan laughingly let herself out into the herb garden, finding the mint with no trouble. She might have lived the first nine years of her life in a town, but she had soon picked up the country ways and knowledge. She and Brian had been much happier here, having room to play, clean air to breathe. It was for the clean air they had come here if they had but known it, their father's illness being irritated by the town smog.

As she stood up she saw Roddy Meyers looking out at her from one of the upstairs windows, turning angrily away as he dared to grin at her. She would wipe that smile off his face when she met him this afternoon!

Her mother was looking slightly better when she got home at lunchtime, although Megan insisted she stay in bed.

'How did you get on, love?' her mother asked worriedly.

'Just fine. They're a bit short-staffed today, so I offered to stay on, but Mrs Reece said they would be able to manage.' Much to her chagrin. If she could have worked this afternoon she would have had a good excuse not to meet Roddy.

'That was nice of you, dear,' she smiled. 'How did you get on with Freda and Mrs Reece?'

Megan shrugged. 'Freda's nice, but I hardly saw Mrs Reece, she was busy organising the cleaning of the house.'

'It's lovely now, isn't it? Now that everywhere has been cleaned up and redecorated.'

'It's all right,' Megan agreed grudgingly, aware that Jerome Towers had been responsible for the improvements. 'Although old Squire Towers always made it seem homely.'

'It's homely now, Megan. And it will be even more so when they get a couple of children running around.'

This conjured up pictures of two small children, tall for their age, a boy and a girl, with their father's dark hair and eyes. They would be lovely children, they would have to be if they looked anything like Jerome Towers.

'Is Mr Towers thinking of getting married?' she asked casually. Being away at the hospital she had missed out on a lot of the local gossip this last year, most of it history by the time she came home for a couple of days, and so not related to her.

'Well, he does have a girl-friend in London. She's been to The Towers for a couple of weekends—a beautiful little thing, very friendly, with red hair.'

'Little thing' rankled. Being five feet eight in her stockinged feet Megan often found herself towering over other women. She would certainly never be the sort of girl men felt protective towards. 'Did Brian borrow the tractor from The Towers?' she changed the subject.

'I think so, dear,' her mother said vaguely. 'I passed the message on anyway. He's called Taylor out from the garage to look at it.'

'Right,' Megan stood up. 'I'll get you some lunch. I—er—I have to go out later. I shouldn't be long,' she added hastily. Just long enough to tell Roddy Meyers that she wouldn't agree to his blackmail a second time.

'Are you going out with one of your friends?' her mother asked interestedly.

'Er—yes.' Although she would hardly call Roddy Meyers a friend—a few other choice names, but certainly not friend.

'That's good, dear.' Mrs Finch closed her eyes. 'I was feeling rather guilty about lying here and leaving you so much on your own.'

'I'm not here to be entertained, Mum,' Megan chided. 'I'm here to work now.'

'You're sure there's no chance of them taking you back at the hospital?'

'Not unless that boy tells them the truth. And as he's already left the hospital I don't think there's any like-lihood of that.' Besides, Roddy's attitude this morning to her dismissal had pointed to him not giving a damn.

'It's such a shame,' her mother frowned. 'You've wanted to be a nurse ever since you were a little girl.'

'Yes,' Megan agreed grimly. 'Still,' she added brightly, 'we can't have everything we want in life. And maybe now that I'm home I can be of some help to Brian.'

'Field work isn't for a girl, Megan. What we need is another man.'

'Well, you'll just have to take what you can get,' Megan told her lightly, 'and that's me!'

'You haven't thought any more about selling to Mr Towers?'

Her mouth tightened. 'I don't need to think about it.

I wouldn't sell to him if I were destitute.'

'We aren't far off that,' sighed her mother.

'Don't be silly,' Megan said briskly. 'All it needs is hard work and——'

'And don't you think Brian has been working hard?' her usually even-tempered mother became angry. 'Do you think we both haven't? But it isn't enough. We can't manage any more.'

'But if I——'

'It isn't enough, Megan,' her mother repeated firmly. 'Your father left the farm and land between the three of us, but I don't think he intended for it to be a millstone around our necks. He knew I'd always have a home with your Aunt Rose, as soon as I'd got you two children off my hands, of course, and——'

'Thanks!' Megan said dryly.

'Well, I expect you'll get married one day.'

'I expect.'

Her mother gave her an impatient look. 'Well, you will, you're a beautiful girl—even if I do say so myself.'

'Dad always said I got my beauty from you,' Megan smiled mischievously.

Her mother blushed. 'So he did,' she agreed in a choked voice. 'Anyway, I'm sure your father intended for us to sell the farm back to Mr Towers, in fact he said as much before he died. He wanted us to use the money as we wanted. Oh, I know Brian wanted to give it a year's trial, see how he managed.' She sighed. 'I think it's pretty obvious that he can't manage at all.'

'So you want to sell?' Megan asked dully.

'I do,' her mother nodded. 'And I think Brian would too if he could find himself a job in this area. Joyce wouldn't want to move too far away from her parents.'

Joyce was Brian's girl-friend of two years, and they were planning to marry soon. As far as Megan knew it could be the financial state of the farm that was holding up those plans.

'I think you should talk this over with Brian, Megan,' her mother advised.

'Maybe I will, Mum. Later, perhaps.' If Brian really wanted to sell she would have no choice but to agree. But to sell out to Rome—*Jerome* Towers, that she wouldn't like.

She was still thoughtful when she met Roddy Meyers later that afternoon, although his triumphant smile made her burn with anger and her eyes glow a deep sparkling green. 'You needn't look so pleased with yourself,' she snapped as he handed her into the low dark green sports car. 'I'm not here through choice,' she added moodily, resisting the impulse to turn and look at The Towers, telling herself she didn't really want to catch a glimpse of Jerome Towers.

Roddy turned to grin at her. 'But you are here.'

'Yes!' Megan snapped.

He accelerated the car out on to the narrow, winding road. 'Where shall we go?'

'Here is far enough, I think,' she told him rigidly. 'I only agreed to meet you so that I can tell you I won't be forced into meeting you again.'

'Forced, Megan?' He raised one blond eyebrow.

'Yes, forced! You knew I wouldn't want your brother to hear about the trouble I had at the hospital, that I wouldn't want anyone to know,' she added hastily as she saw the speculative look in his eyes.

'But you specifically mentioned Rome,' he said thoughtfully. 'Why him especially?'

'I only mentioned him because he happened to be the witness to your blackmail,' she said awkwardly. 'I like your brother even less than I like you—and we both know my feelings towards you.'

They were still driving, the high hedges making it impossible for them to see anything but the road in front of them. It gave them an intimacy Megan found irksome.

'You looked like another of the fatalities to Rome's charm to me,' Roddy scorned. 'You hated him seeing you in my arms.'

'I hated *being* in your arms,' she corrected forcefully. 'Your brother's presence there was irrelevant.'

'You're a liar, Megan Finch,' Roddy told her harshly. 'I don't know what it is about Rome, but the women go down like ninepins whenever he's around.'

'My mother tells me he has a girl-friend in London.' In which case he had no right to have asked *her* out— even if he had changed his mind.

'She must mean Stella,' Roddy said knowingly. 'She's been Rome's woman for over a year now.'

'His *woman*!' Megan spluttered. 'My God, what a charming description,' she said disgustedly.

'But a true one. Stella wouldn't mind, she likes being his woman. She would probably like to be his wife too, but Rome doesn't go in for permanent relationships.'

'A year sounds pretty permanent to me.'

'And me,' Roddy grinned. 'But one day Stella will wake up and find Rome has just eliminated her from his life. She'll keep calling him, crying all over the place, pleading for him to come back to her, and he'll just ignore her as if he never knew her. I've seen it all before, many times. I've even got myself a couple of girl-friends that way.'

'He sounds a right swine,' and she was well out of the situation! thought Megan.

'I'm his one weak spot,' Roddy told her with satisfaction. 'Rome can see no wrong in his little brother.'

'Meaning?' her eyes narrowed suspiciously.

'Meaning that even if you told him the truth about what had happened at the hospital he wouldn't believe you. Rome's opinion of women isn't too hot.'

'You mean he's never caught you in a compromising situation, never caught you trying to force some other poor girl into bed with you?' Megan scorned him, angry with both men. 'Not even Patsy?' she asked softly.

Hot colour stained his cheeks. 'What do you know about her?'

'I know that she's newly married, that she's frightened to work at the house while you're there. What did you do to the poor girl?'

'Nothing,' he said moodily. 'And I don't see that it's any of your business anyway.'

Megan shook her head. 'Why don't you choose a woman who's attracted to you in return?'

'Who says she isn't?' he asked sneeringly.

'I do. Patsy's only been married six months, I doubt she's interested in extra-marital affairs just yet.'

Roddy gave an unpleasant smile. 'Every woman is interested in an affair, married or not.'

'The trouble with you, Roddy,' Megan taunted, 'is that you think every girl is playing hard to get. Well, I wasn't, and I'm still not interested. Now I won't tell your brother anything about you, Roddy, if you don't tell him anything about me. I think it's a case of mutual silence.'

'Maybe,' he agreed consideringly. 'Does that mean you aren't going to go out with me?'

'It means,' she controlled her anger with difficulty, 'that I want you to stay away from me. You've already ruined my career, I don't want you to do any more damage to my life. No one knows, not my family or anyone, that you're the man involved in my dismissal. I'd like it to stay that way. Will it?'

'I suppose so,' he gave a grudging nod.

Megan heaved an inward sigh of relief; one of her problems was solved at least. 'Right, well you can take me back now.'

Roddy gave her a sulky look. 'You could at least go out with me now you're here.'

'I've said what I want to say—No, perhaps I haven't said it all. If you dare to tell anyone about those incidents at the hospital I'll make sure your brother knows the truth—about myself and Patsy. We can't both be lying.'

'God, you're a hard little bitch!'

'You get that way when your reputation is in shreds, when even your own family isn't quite sure you're telling the truth,' she recalled bitterly. It had taken some time to convince Brian, although her mother had instantly believed her.

'For God's sake,' Roddy snapped, 'I've said I'm sorry!'

'No, you haven't,' she contradicted. 'But even if you had it wouldn't make things any different, only telling the hospital authorities could do that.'

'Which I'm certainly not going to do,' Roddy scorned. 'Rome would be sure to find out, and he would stop my allowance—among other things,' he grimaced.

'At your age you should be out at work earning your own money, not sponging on your brother.'

'God, what a nag you are!'

'Aren't you glad I refused to go out with you?' she taunted. 'You can take me back to The Towers. I have to see Mrs Reece. The housekeeper,' she added.

'I know who she is,' he said moodily.

The drive back was completed in silence. After droppping Megan off outside the house Roddy accelerated the car back out of the driveway at such speed that some of the small stones flew high into the air.

Megan found Mrs Reece in the kitchen taking her afternoon tea. And if this afternoon had been as hectic as this morning had been then the poor woman was much in need of it. Megan had promised the house-keeper she would pop in to see whether or not Patsy would be in tomorrow. She had offered to come in all day herself if the other girl was to be absent again.

'She isn't coming back at all,' Mrs Reece told her with a sigh. 'Apparently her Donald has decided he doesn't want her to work any more.'

Roddy had done a good job of frightening the other girl away. Donald Jones was a possessive boy, and the slightest sign of interest in Patsy from another man would be enough for him to stop her coming here any more.

'Well, I could come in for a few days full-time,' Megan offered. 'Just until you get someone else.'

'Could you?' Mrs Reece accepted gratefully. She was a middle-aged woman of perhaps fifty, her hair already snow-white, her figure neat and trim, her energy bound-less.

'Just for a while,' Megan nodded. 'I——'

The door leading to the main part of the house was suddenly thrown open, and the new owner stood looking at them. Megan jumped almost guiltily to her feet, al-though Mrs Reece and Freda seemed unconcerned.

Velvety brown eyes passed insolently over Megan's denim-clad figure, over the way the green sweater hugged her breasts and the flatness of her stomach. Megan felt as if he were mentally undressing her—and liking what he saw! She looked sharply at the other two women in the room, but they seemed unaware of her boss's appraisal.

'Roddy told me I would find you in here,' Jerome Towers spoke to her.

So he was back already! 'I called in to see Mrs Reece,' she answered resentfully.

'He told me that too,' he drawled. 'I just wanted you to pass on a message to your brother. Tell him I'll call in this evening. I have some things I want to discuss with him.'

Megan bristled angrily at his autocratic tone. 'If it's anything to do with the farm you can discuss it with me.'

His gaze ran over her coldly, contemptuously. 'Women have their uses,' he told her insultingly. 'And being in business isn't one of them. Tell Brian I'll be there about eight-thirty.' He left as abruptly as he had entered.

CHAPTER THREE

SHE relayed the message to her brother, watching the worried frown that marred his brow.

'I wonder what he wants,' Brian said thoughtfully.

'I have no idea,' Megan told him crossly. 'He wouldn't tell me.'

'Did you ask him?'

'Yes.'

Brian grinned at her anger. 'By the way, Jeff said he hadn't had time this morning to come out and look at our tractor, but that Mr Towers told him to let us borrow one of theirs. How did Mr Towers know about it?'

Megan explained her mistake, although she omitted

the fact that Jerome Towers had invited her out to dinner, and also that he had changed his mind when he realised she was his own hired help. 'It was a natural mistake to make,' she added moodily.

'Oh yes,' Brian chuckled. 'Jeff and Mr Towers really look alike. Jeff is about my height, with red hair,' he explained. 'Mr Towers must be all of six and a half feet, with hair as black as coal.'

'Well, I didn't know that!' No wonder her mother had been surprised when she had said she thought 'Jeff' was good-looking! 'I didn't expect the famous—or do I mean *in*famous?—Mr Towers to bring Bertha back here himself.'

Brian shrugged. 'I doubt there was anyone else to do it. They were very busy over there this morning, Jeff had to stay with a sick cow, and the other workers were probably out on the estate.'

'I wasn't to know that,' she groaned. 'Oh, I felt such a fool when I found out the truth.'

'I'd better get washed.' Brian stood up from the dinner table. 'And I'd better telephone Joyce and tell her I could be over rather late tonight,' he grimaced.

Megan went in to collect her mother's tray, to find most of the stew eaten. 'Feeling better?' she asked gently.

'Quite a bit,' her mother nodded. 'You're spoiling me, Megan. I can't remember the last time I was coddled like this.'

'Neither can I, which is why I intend seeing you stay in bed until you're better. I'm going to be working full-time at The Towers for the next week or so, but I'll be able to come home and get your lunch for you,' Megan promised.

'You needn't bother to do that, love, I can get up and get myself some soup or something. What's Brian so happy about?' He could be heard whistling in his bedroom. 'Is everywhere tidy?' her mother wanted to know as soon as she knew Jerome Towers was to come here this evening.

'Yes,' Megan sighed. 'I made sure of that when I got back this afternoon. Now you get some sleep, you're looking tired.'

Her mother was frowning. 'If you give him tea or coffee make sure you use the best china. And——'

'Stop worrying, Mum!' Megan laughed. 'I'll make sure I don't disgrace you.'

'It isn't that,' her mother flushed. 'It's just that Mr Towers is a nice young man, always kind to me whenever he sees me in the house, and I want to show him the same politeness.'

'All right, Mum,' Megan sighed. 'I'll be extra polite to him.' If he would let her! He seemed to go out of his way to deliberately antagonise her every time they met.

Their farmhouse might be small, but it was always kept scrupulously clean and tidy, flowers always brightening up the shabbiness of the lounge, the log fire that she had lit also giving the place a bright cheerfulness that was sadly lacking on a cold frosty morning.

Brian was on the telephone to Joyce when Jerome Towers arrived at exactly eight-thirty, and so it was left to Megan to open the door to him. He was dressed in thigh-hugging cream trousers and matching jacket, and a fitted roll-necked brown sweater. He looked very attractive—and was probably well aware of the fact.

'Would you like to come in?' she invited.

His eyes mocked her. 'That was the idea of the visit,' he drawled, and followed her into the lounge, ducking his head as he came through the doorway, then straightening as he entered the room, his dark head almost touching the low ceiling beams.

'Brian won't be a moment.' Her voice was stilted in her effort to be polite, as once again he instantly annoyed her. 'He's on the telephone in the other room,' she explained.

'That's all right. May I sit down?' He quirked one dark eyebrow at her.

'Oh—er—yes. Please do.' She watched as he sat down in one of the comfortable armchairs that stood beside the fire, seating herself in the one opposite him. 'My brother and I, and of course my mother, have equal shares in this farm, and so whatever you want to talk to Brian about can be discussed just as well with me.'

'I don't think so,' he dismissed, turning away.

Megan flushed angrily. 'You may want to dismiss women from business, Mr Towers,' she snapped, 'but as far as this farm goes the majority of it belongs to females.'

'I believe I'm right in saying that your mother shares Brian's view that the farm should be sold,' he said coldly.

'But I don't!' Her eyes flashed. 'This farm is my home.'

'Until a few days ago you couldn't give a damn about this place. You were living quite happily in Redford,' he scorned. 'With no idea of coming back here.'

'That isn't true!' she flashed her resentment. 'I've always regarded the farm as my home.'

'There's no reason why it shouldn't remain so,' he told her in a bored voice. 'I'm only interested in the land.'

'Why?'

'Why?' He frowned his puzzlement at her question.

'I'm sure your brother has already explained my reasons.'

'He may have done,' Megan nodded, 'but I'm more interested in your version of it.'

His eyes narrowed. 'I've told you before, I don't believe a woman's place is in business.'

'Your brother explained to me your idea of a woman's place,' Megan said with distaste.

Jerome Towers' expression lightened. 'I'm sure you didn't agree with it,' he drawled.

'No, I didn't! You——'

Brian came into the lounge. 'You should have told me Mr Towers was here,' he told Megan with a certain amount of impatience. 'I was only talking to Joyce.'

'I'm sure she wouldn't like being dismissed in that casual way,' Megan defended her future sister-in-law.

Jerome Towers stood up, shaking Brian's proffered hand, and instantly dwarfing the other man. 'Could we perhaps go to your study and talk?' he suggested smoothly.

Megan glared at him, her green eyes blazing. 'Don't bother,' she snapped. 'I'm going now. Goodbye, Mr Towers.'

He looked down his haughty nose at her. 'I would like to talk to you too later.'

'I'm sorry,' she refused sharply, 'I'm going out for the evening.'

'Megan——'

'I'll see you later,' she interrupted her brother's protest, and slammed out of the room.

Damn the man! Now she would have to go out, even though she had had no intention of doing so. She would go and see Wendy, a friend since schooldays, and her brother Paul, who was also a friend.

Wendy and Paul were up in Wendy's bedroom listening to records when Megan arrived, and they expressed surprise at seeing her home again so soon after her last days off. She told them the truth about her reason for being back, although she once again omitted the fact that Roddy Meyers was the man involved.

'So we have a femme fatale in our midst,' Paul joked; he was a tall dark-haired man of twenty-two, with laughing blue eyes and an easygoing nature. He and Megan often dated when she was at home, although it had never developed into anything serious on either side. They just enjoyed each other's company.

'Stop it, Paul,' reprimanded his young sister, a pretty girl with her brother's dark colouring. 'Can't you see Megan is upset about it? You know how she's always wanted to be a nurse.'

'I remember I used to love playing her patient when we were kids,' Paul teased. 'I used to get injuries in the most curious places,' he grinned, 'just so that Megan could bandage me up.'

Megan couldn't help smiling. 'I used to realise what you were up to and bandage you up so tight that you couldn't move.'

He grimaced. 'So you did. I'd forgotten that bit. How on earth did you get involved with a louse like that man at the hospital? Couldn't you see what he was up to?'

'Oh, I could see all right, I just thought I could handle it.'

'Well, now that you're here,' Wendy smiled, 'Paul can take us both down to the local for a pint.'

'So I can drown my sorrows?' Megan laughed. 'I think I may need to after tonight. Jerome Towers is at the farm talking to Brian,' she explained, 'and I think he's up to something.'

'So you've finally met him,' Wendy said eagerly.

'Oh no!' Paul groaned. 'Now look what you've started,' he told Megan accusingly. 'She'll go into raptures about the man now!'

'I won't,' his sister said crossly.

'She will,' Paul moaned knowingly.

Wendy picked up a pillow and threw it at him. He ducked, and it hit the wall behind him and slid to the floor. 'Having to look at your ugly mug every day I'm not surprised I think Jerome Towers is fantastic-looking,' she glared at him.

'Here we go!' Paul raised his eyes heavenwards.

'Well, he is. And he's so sexy—he just oozes sex-appeal.'

'I didn't notice,' Megan drawled. She had noticed when she first met him, but her opinion had changed on further acquaintance. He was a conceited swine, and she didn't like him.

'Does that mean you don't fancy him?' Paul asked eagerly.

'That's right, I don't.'

He grinned. 'Thank God for a sensible female at last! I'm much more your taste, aren't I, Megan love?'

She laughed. 'You could be.'

He grimaced. 'That's all I ever get from you, half promises.'

'I don't know why she goes out with you at all,' Wendy taunted her brother. 'I would have credited her with more sense.'

Megan listened to their lighthearted bantering on the drive to the pub, the three of them crowded into Paul's battered sports car, the canvas roof back to give them more room, in spite of the cold.

Wendy groaned as she climbed out, holding her back

in exaggerated pain. 'What a crate!' She playfully kicked one of the wheels.

Paul grinned. 'I was very comfortable. I don't mind Megan squashing up against me any day of the week.' He put his arm about her shoulders as they entered the pub.

After the battering Megan had taken the last few days it was good to relax with someone as uncomplicated as Paul Carter. They joined several of their other friends in the pub, laughing and joking together until closing time.

'I'm going home with Bill,' Wendy told them.

Paul frowned, suddenly serious. 'Bill Pope?'

'Yes.'

'Okay,' he nodded. 'I suppose he's trustworthy.'

Wendy looked indignant. 'Even if he weren't it would be none of your business. I don't pass comments on the people you date.'

'That's because I only date Megan,' he said confidently. 'And she happens to be your best friend.'

'Ooh, you're so smug!' Wendy flounced off.

Megan laughed, giving Paul a rueful look. 'One of these days . . .' she warned.

'I know,' he grimaced, unlocking the car door for her. 'She's actually going to hit me. But until that happens I'll continue to protect her, even if she doesn't like it.'

'Hey, Paul,' another couple came out of the pub, walking over to the car. 'Could you give us a lift?' Noel asked.

'Sure,' Paul agreed instantly. 'Although you'll have to sit in the back, and I have it on good authority that it isn't the most comfortable of seats.'

'As long as we don't have to walk.' Noel and his girl-friend Ginny clambered into the back, perching precariously on the trunk of the car.

Noel started singing one of his crude rugby songs part way through the drive, and pretty soon Paul had joined in. Megan and Ginny laughed uproariously at the outrageousness of some of the words.

'Oh hell!' Paul had time to shout before he swerved the car to miss something that had run into the road in front of them.

The car came to a screeching halt several yards farther down the road, and all of them got out to run back and see if they had actually hit anything. Just as they reached the spot a man strode angrily out of a neighbouring field, and even in the poor light his expression could be seen as thunderous. A dog sat at his heels, a golden labrador, her tongue hanging out as she panted, turning her head to look up adoringly at her master.

'You bloody hooligans!' Jerome Towers snapped furiously. 'You almost ran my dog over. It may have escaped your notice, but the speed limit around here is thirty miles an hour, and you must have been doing all of fifty. And you were making enough noise to wake up the whole damned village!' he added with violence.

'In that case,' Megan stepped forward, 'why didn't you call your dog to heel? You must have realised we were travelling down this road.'

Glacial brown eyes were turned on her. 'Oh, it's you, is it!' the words were almost an accusation. 'I might have known you would be involved in this somewhere!'

Hot colour stained her cheeks at her friends' speculative looks, although of course they couldn't see that in the darkness. 'You might own The Towers, and *most* of the land around it, Mr Towers,' she said pointedly, 'but you don't own this road, and so consequently we have

more right to be on it than your dog does.' Loving ani-
mals as she did she would have felt terrible if anything
had happened to this beautiful golden labrador, but her
point was valid, even if it sounded heartless.

Those brown eyes were narrowed now, and Megan
wondered how she could ever have thought them warm
and velvety. His expression was contemptuous, dismis-
sing her before he turned to look at Paul. 'I'm warning
you, Carter,' his voice was dangerously soft, 'any repeat
of this incident and I'll make sure the police get to hear
about it. Next time it might be a human being, and you
might not miss. And before you make the obvious
comeback, Miss Finch,' he added coldly, 'I'll make sure
it isn't me.'

'Shame!' Megan muttered vehemently.

'The feeling is mutual,' he drawled insultingly, then
turned on his heel and walked away, the dog walking
obediently at his side.

'Wow!' Paul breathed slowly. 'The local lord of the
manor, no less!'

'You didn't pull your punches, Megan,' Ginny giggled
as they all got back into the car.

'I can't stand the man!' she said through gritted teeth.

'No, you can't, can you,' Paul said thoughtfully. 'Why
can't you?' he asked once they had dropped off the other
couple and were parked outside Megan's home.

She shrugged. 'I just don't like him.' Her eyes teased
as she looked at him. 'Maybe I just prefer young farm-
workers who play rugby on a Saturday and go to church
on a Sunday.'

'That's what I like to hear.' He put his arms around
her and pulled her towards him. 'Exactly what I like to
hear,' he murmured before his lips claimed hers.

Always in the past Megan had enjoyed Paul's kisses,
and she enjoyed them now, but at the back of her mind

was the memory of finely chiselled lips exploring hers with intimate thoroughness. Paul finally pulled back, sensing her preoccupation.

'Anything wrong?' he asked huskily.

'No, nothing,' her smile was bright. 'Maybe I'm still suffering from nerves where—where that man tried to force me.'

'God, yes!' he groaned. 'I'm sorry, love. How damned thoughtless of me!'

'Not at all,' she hastened to reassure him. 'Would you like to come in for coffee?' she offered, feeling guilty about deceiving him. Roddy Meyers had angered her, but he certainly hadn't frightened her.

'I think I'd better.' Paul grimaced, looking up at the darkly clouded sky. 'It's just starting to rain.'

They got a soaking while trying to put up the canvas roof on the car, although Megan didn't mind. She couldn't help hoping that Jerome Towers had got caught in the storm; he had only been wearing denims and a light rollnecked sweater. He had been quite a way from The Towers, and had, she hoped, got wet. Rude, insufferable man!

'Whew!' Paul warmed himself in front of the fire, shivering slightly.

'I'll just check on Mum and then I'll get us that coffee.' Megan disappeared down the passageway to her mother's bedroom.

All was in darkness inside, the fire in here having burnt down quite low. Megan added more logs before replacing the fireguard. Her mother was still fast asleep, her breathing a little easier than it had been before Megan went out, so she quietly crept out of the room. Her mother must be in a deep sleep, usually the slightest sound woke her up. Megan could remember numerous occasions when she had tried to creep into the house when late home, only to find her mother wide awake and demanding an explanation.

'Here we are.' She put their mugs of coffee on the table, having already sugared Paul's.

'Lovely!' He sat down beside her on the sofa. 'This man, the one at the hospital, did he——'

'Heavens, no!' Megan hastily denied, knowing what he was going to ask. 'It was all just very unpleasant.'

'He wants flattening,' Paul growled.

She laughed, 'You sound like Brian!'

'I probably feel like Brian. If I ever met him ... What's his name?' he probed.

'Er—Oh, damn!' She deliberately tipped coffee on her denim-clad legs, hoping to divert Paul away from the subject of Roddy Meyers. By the time she had mopped up the hot liquid with a cloth from the kitchen she seemed to have succeeded, although the coffee hadn't done her denims much good.

Paul drank the remains of his own coffee. 'I'd better be going. I have to be up early in the morning. Unless, of course, my boss has decided I'm too much of a hooligan to employ any more. Especially when my girlfriend told him she would rather it was him we'd nearly run over,' he added teasingly.

'Oh God!' Megan groaned. 'I forgot you work for Jerome Towers.'

'It's all right, love,' he grinned. 'He isn't the type to let that influence him. I was just teasing you. It isn't like you to take such a dislike to someone.'

'You aren't telling me you actually like him?'

Paul shrugged. 'I don't dislike him. I must say he's very——'

'Fair,' Megan finished scornfully. 'So everyone keeps telling me.'

'My, my, you do dislike him! Come on, you can

see me to the door.'

They were kissing on the doorstep when Brian arrived home, and Megan moved almost guiltily away from Paul. It seemed strange for her big brother to see her kissing someone.

'Don't mind me,' he grinned, as he went past them into the farmhouse.

'I'd better go in,' Megan said awkwardly, wanting to ask Brian about Jerome Towers' visit earlier tonight.

Paul still had his arms about her waist. 'Are you coming to the dance with me on Saturday?'

'I suppose so,' she smiled. The 'dance' consisted of an evening spent at the local village hall, with a young band trying to play all types of music because there were always people of all ages there, young and old. It was really just an excuse for all the locals to get together for a chat, but at least it was an evening out, in an area where there was little entertainment. 'I'll look forward to it,' she assured him.

She found Brian in the kitchen preparing himself some coffee. 'What did Mr Towers want?' She came straight to the point.

Her brother shrugged. 'He had a proposition to put to me, a very interesting one as it happens.'

Megan frowned. 'What sort of proposition?'

He sipped his hot drink. 'A very sensible one,' he said thoughtfully.

'Well?' She looked at him expectantly.

Brian sighed. 'You want to know about it, don't you?'

'Of course I do! I am still a member of this family, you know. I may be a disgraced member at the moment, but——'

'Don't be silly, Megan,' Brian dismissed angrily. 'I hope you haven't been telling Paul about that little episode.'

She flushed. 'I told him. It's all right, Brian,' she assured him, 'Paul won't tell anyone.'

'He'd better not. We may just be lucky and no one else will get to hear about it.'

'It's my reputation that will be in shreds, not yours,' Megan told him resentfully.

'Your reputation with Mr Towers is likely to be in shreds anyway after your behaviour this evening. Why on earth were you so rude to him?'

'I wasn't rude,' she said moodily. 'Or if I was,' she added grudgingly at Brian's sceptical look, 'he was rude to me first.'

'Don't be childish, Megan. You deliberately went out tonight because you knew he wanted to talk to you. I just hope it hasn't jeopardised his offer to help us.'

'Help us?' She gave her brother a sharp look. 'How could the arrogant Jerome Towers help us?'

'No way, not if you keep up this attitude. The whole thing depends on your co-operation, and the mood you're in at the moment you aren't going to be co-operative about anything.'

She frowned. '*My* co-operation? What does his plan have to do with me?'

Brian picked up his mug of coffee and walked to the door. 'I'm not allowed to tell you,' he said lightly. 'See you in the morning. Is Mum okay, by the way?'

'Yes, she's fine, she's asleep actually. But——'

'Good.'

'Brian!' She caught up with him at the bottom of the stairs. 'You can't just walk away like this.'

'I'm tired, Megan,' he yawned as if to prove the point. 'And I've got a long day ahead of me tomorrow.'

'But—Brian!' she repeated crossly as he walked away again.

'Keep your voice down,' he told her in a fierce whisper. 'You'll wake Mum up.'

'But why aren't you allowed to tell me?'

'Mr Towers thought it might be better if he talked to you about it himself, and I'm inclined to agree with him. Just remember, Megan, we need all the help we can get.'

She frowned. 'I'll remember.'

She was woken once in the night by her mother's racking cough, making her a hot drink and sitting with her until she fell asleep again. By that time Megan was well and truly awake, so she stayed up to get Brian's early morning cup of tea. Not that she got any further information out of him, Brian being one of those people who were totally uncommunicative first thing in the morning.

Freda asked her to take in the breakfast things when she arrived at The Towers, and the trays of bacon, sausages, and scrambled eggs made Megan's mouth water.

'Is Mr Towers a late riser too?' she scorned.

'Oh no, love,' Freda put the hot toast in the rack. 'He's been up and about the estate since six o'clock, like he is every morning. He just finds it more convenient to eat this time of day.'

'Is Rod—er—Mr Meyers still here?' Megan inwardly cursed herself for that slip.

'Yes, he's still here. Take these through, love,' the cook put the tray of food in her hand, 'before it all gets cold.'

The breakfast-room was as gracious as the rest of the house, with wood-panelled walls, and the oak table was already set for two people—Jerome Towers and Roddy Meyers, both men she heartily disliked.

The door opened behind her and she turned almost

guiltily. 'Oh, it's you,' she said ungraciously.

Roddy Meyers sauntered over to her. 'Is that any way to greet me, darling?' he drawled, standing uncomfortably close to her.

'What did you expect?' she scorned, ignoring the endearment, knowing it was as false as the rest of the man. 'A kiss?'

'That's not a bad idea,' he said softly, his head swooping as his mouth claimed hers.

'When you've quite finished . . .' rasped a coldly angry voice.

Megan began to struggle in earnest, but Roddy took his time removing his lips from hers, then turned to look at his brother. 'Morning, Rome,' he grinned. 'Can you think of a better way to start the morning?'

Jerome Towers' gaze swept scathingly over Megan's flushed features, passing insultingly over the soft curves of her body in the full scarlet skirt and black drawstring blouse she wore. 'Yes, I can think of a much better way,' his tone implied that it would be more intimate, 'but with all the men Miss Finch already has in her life I doubt she would be able to fit me into her social calendar.'

Roddy looked down at the furious Megan. '*Men*, Megan?' he taunted. 'And I thought I was the only one!'

Her eyes flashed. 'You——'

'Perhaps you could fetch our coffee, Miss Finch?' Jerome Towers requested icily, and sat down at the table, very lithe and attractive in close-fitting denims that emphasised the long length of his muscular legs, the brown shirt stretched tautly across his wide shoulders. 'Unless, of course, you can't bear to tear yourself away from my brother's arms?' he quirked a mocking eyebrow.

She pulled away from Roddy. 'I can do that quite easily,' she snapped, glaring at them both.

'That wasn't what you said last night,' Roddy drawled suggestively.

Megan gasped. 'Last night——? But I——'

'The coffee, Miss Finch,' reminded that cold, infuriating voice.

She gave one last glare at Roddy before flouncing out of the room. What game was Roddy playing now?

'Coffee,' Freda put the pot on the tray for her. 'Strong and black, the way Mr Towers likes it.'

'Will I be expected to stay and pour it?' More and more Megan was beginning to regret this offer to help out for a few days.

'Oh no, love,' Freda gave one of her beaming smiles, 'Mr Towers doesn't like a lot of waiting on.'

It seemed to Megan that in the short time he had been here 'Mr Towers' had made his likes and dislikes well known. Well, as far as she was concerned *he* was one of *her* dislikes!

Roddy was on his own when she returned to the breakfast room. 'Rome was called to the telephone,' he explained his brother's absence at her puzzled look.

She banged the coffee-pot down on the table. 'What did you mean about last night? she demanded to know. 'I didn't even see you last night.'

'No, well—You see, the—er—lady I was with last night—well, Rome wouldn't approve of my seeing her.'

'He doesn't approve of me either,' she said dryly. 'Anyway, he saw me out with someone else last night.'

'Who?' Roddy asked sharply.

'Mind your own damned business!'

He drew a ragged breath. 'What time did Rome see you?'

'About elevenish, I suppose.'

'Oh, that's all right, then. I was back home by ten o'clock. The—person I was seeing had to be home early, and Rome knows what time I got in.' He gave her a considering look. 'Aren't you interested in who I saw last night? If you asked me I might just tell you.'

'I'm not interested,' Megan snapped. 'What I am interested in is the fact that your brother now thinks I saw you *and* Paul last night.'

Roddy grinned. 'Mm, I suppose he does.'

'Thank you very much!'

He shrugged. 'Does it matter?'

'Of course it damn well matters. Why should I cover up for you? You've caused me nothing but trouble since I first met you.'

'Oh, come on, Megan,' he soothed. 'What does it matter what Rome thinks of you? You obviously don't like him.'

'The fact that I dislike *Rome*,' she scorned, 'has nothing to do——'

'The fact that you dislike me, Miss Finch,' Jerome Towers came unhurriedly back into the room, 'doesn't mean you are at liberty to call me Rome, however sarcastically. Only close friends and relatives are allowed that privilege.' He gave her a cold look. 'And you aren't either of those things.'

Her eyes flashed like emeralds. 'And have no wish to be,' she snapped. 'I was merely quoting your brother. I believe you want to speak to me, *Mr Towers*.'

'Not right now,' he dismissed, helping himself to the food on the sidetable. 'I never discuss business on an empty stomach. I'll call for you later today.'

'Yes, sir,' Megan bit out furiously. 'If that's all, sir?' She was tempted to curtsey, his arrogance so infuriated her.

Those dark brown eyes were glacial. 'That is all,

Miss Finch—until later.'

'Yes, sir!' She walked stiffly to the door, Roddy Meyers' obvious amusement only succeeding in making her more angry.

'And, Miss Finch——' that softly taunting voice halted her at the door, 'if you call me sir just once more,' he said as she turned, 'I'll carry out that service you said the Squire was no longer entitled to.'

'Oh!' The door slammed behind her as she hurried back to the kitchen.

Fool, she cursed herself. He wouldn't really carry out that threat, he was just trying to unnerve her. And he had succeeded! That only made her resentment all the stronger.

She had helped Mrs Reece tidy the house and was polishing the silver in the kitchen when Jerome Towers 'called' for her.

In fact he came for her himself, walking into the kitchen as suddenly as he had yesterday, grinning at Freda as he helped himself to one of the freshly baked cakes cooling on a tray. 'Mm, as delicious as usual,' he gave the cook a warm smile, then his features became harsh as he looked at Megan. 'I have time to talk to you now,' he informed her coldly.

'I have the silver to finish,' she refused tautly.

'Oh, that can wait, Megan,' Freda told her with a smile. 'You run along with Mr Towers.'

'Run along' just about described it. Jerome Towers made no concessions for her smaller steps as he strode along to his study. Megan found herself facing him across the desk.

'Brian said you have some way of helping us,' she said bluntly, refusing to sit down.

'You sound as if you doubt it,' he drawled mockingly.

'I don't have any reason to presume you would genuinely want to help us.'

His eyes narrowed, his masculine vitality a tangible thing in the confines of this small room. 'You don't have any reason to think the opposite either,' he rasped.

'Of course I do,' she scorned. 'With our land The Towers estate would be back intact.'

'You seem to be obsessed with that idea,' he sighed.

'Can you deny it's true?'

'I wouldn't even attempt to try when you seem so convinced of it.'

'Your proposal, Mr Towers?' she said stiffly.

He sat back in the leather swivel-chair. 'It's quite simple, Miss Finch. Your brother needs help working the land——'

'Once my mother is feeling better I'll be able to help him.'

He looked at her slenderness. 'Forgive my saying so, but you look as if you would be more of a hindrance than a help around a farm. I've offered your brother one of my workers. In exchange——'

'I thought there would have to be an exchange,' Megan taunted.

'In exchange you will come to work for me here at the house,' he finished abruptly.

CHAPTER FOUR

'You have to be joking!' she gasped.

'Do I look as if I'm laughing?' he taunted.

Megan sat down abruptly. 'Come and work here for you?' she repeated dazedly.

Jerome nodded. 'That was the idea.'

'Why?' She eyed him suspiciously.

'I've just explained why—you don't look as if you would be of much help to Brian.'

'I didn't mean that,' she dismissed impatiently. 'I meant why should you want to save me from all that hard work?'

'Would I be doing that?' Jerome mocked. 'I can assure you that wasn't my intention.'

Megan flushed resentfully at his insulting tone. 'Then what was your *intention*?'

'To make sure your farm is kept in line with the rest of the Towers estate.'

'For what purpose?'

He laughed softly. 'So that it's in good order when I eventually persuade you to sell it.'

'I thought as much,' she snapped, standing indignantly to her feet. 'You'll never buy our farm. Never!'

He shrugged, unmoved by her outburst. 'Brian and I decided, if you were agreeable to the scheme, that we would give it six months. If things haven't changed by then your brother has decided to sell out—to me.'

'He had no right to agree to that,' she stormed. 'It should be a family decision.'

'It will be, when I have your yes to the idea. For God's sake, Megan,' he sat forward angrily, 'surely you can see that it's working your brother into the ground itself? Do you want him to die of overwork, as your father did?'

Megan went white. 'My father didn't die of overwork! He was ill before we came here. He——'

'I know, I know,' he sighed. 'I'm sorry I said that. I realise your father came out here for his health, but he would have been better off working in an office or something like that.'

'He wanted to be independent,' she choked. 'To try and make a life, a future, for all of us. You wouldn't understand—' Tears threatened to blind her, and Jerome Towers' dark figure became hazy.

'I do understand, believe me.'

'You couldn't. You've always been rich, always had everything you wanted, always known that The Towers would be yours one day. Whereas we—Let go of me!' she ordered as his arms came about her. She pushed ineffectually at his chest. 'Take your hands off me!'

'No,' he refused huskily, pulling her closer. 'I like you in my arms, Megan. And as you just said, I always get what I want. Right now I want——'

'Let go of me, you—you *womaniser*!' She blinked back her tears to glare at him. 'I suppose you're one of those men with an exaggerated sex-drive,' she accused. 'One of those men who need to take a woman two or three times a week!'

He moved back to sit on the edge of the desk, perfectly relaxed, unmoved by her verbal attack. 'Oh, at least,' he agreed mockingly. 'Two or three times a *week* is an exaggerated sex-drive?' he taunted.

Colour flooded her cheeks. What did she know about such things! 'For an unmarried man it is,' she defended.

'Maybe,' he acknowledged consideringly.

'Well, I don't intend making up this week's quota!'

'From what I've seen the last couple of days you have more than enough men to satisfy your own sex-drive.'

'My own——!' she gasped. 'How dare you! How dare you say such things to me?' She turned on her heel and walked to the door. 'I wouldn't work for you at any price!'

Jerome swung her roughly round to face him. 'You'll work for me,' he told her grimly, 'for no price. I'm not paying you—Paul will be payment enough.'

'Paul?' Her expression brightened. 'Paul Carter will be helping Brian?'

'Yes,' he ground out. 'But that doesn't mean you can spend all your time with him. His time will be fully taken up with the farm, and you will be busy here. If I'd realised he was one of your—special friends,' he drawled the words insultingly, 'I would have chosen someone else. Unfortunately I've already suggested him to Brian, and he's agreed.'

'Oh, good,' Megan smiled happily, enjoying this man's anger. 'Paul's a very good worker,' she added mockingly.

'I know,' Jerome said tautly. 'But don't worry, I intend getting equally good service out of you.'

Megan flushed, not liking the way he had said that. 'In that case, I think I should get back to cleaning the silver.'

'I want it understood,' his firm voice halted her departure, 'that this service does not include visiting my brother's bedroom. In fact, I would prefer it if you didn't go out with him either.'

'Would you indeed?' she said softly. 'Well, I really don't think it's any of your business. Unless you intend making that part of the bargain?'

He had picked up the gold letter-opener from the desk-top, studying it before suddenly looking up, catching her gaze and holding it. 'It isn't part of the bargain, Megan, but a personal request from me.'

'Request denied,' she snapped, angry with herself for noting what nice hands he had, tanned and fleshless, the fingers long and sensitive. He handled the letter-opener with extreme delicacy, and it took a great effort of will on Megan's part to wrench her gaze away. She had been wondering what it would be like to have those hands on her in passion, to feel such delicate caresses on her body, and her face flushed with the embarrassment of her thoughts. She faced him defiantly. 'I'll go out with whoever I want!' There was challenge in her voice, and she almost breathed a sigh of relief when Jerome put the curved letter-opener down on the desk, those beautiful hands resting aimlessly back on the desk-top.

'I've noticed,' he taunted. 'Two men in one night—you really believe in numbers.'

'The more the merrier,' she quipped. 'As long as it doesn't interfere with my work you'll have no reason for complaint.'

'No.' He gave a tight smile. 'I suppose I should feel flattered that you were willing to fit me into your busy schedule yesterday lunchtime.'

'Only because I thought you were Jeff Robbins. If I'd realised who you really where I would have turned you down flat,' she told him insultingly.

'Then perhaps it's as well that I have no intention of repeating the offer,' he scorned.

'The answer would be no even if you did!'

'But I won't.' He smiled at her obvious anger. 'I'm going to enjoy working with you.'

'*With* me?' Megan looked startled. 'I'm going to be working for you, not with you. Unless you intend following me around the house with a duster?' she enquired sweetly.

'God forbid!' he laughed, those brown eyes once more the warm colour of their first meeting, his usually harsh features almost boyish. 'No, I don't intend doing that. Maybe I haven't explained your job function very well. In the afternoons you'll be helping around the house, yes, but in the mornings we'll be working together in here answering my mail and dealing with my social commitments—of which there seem to be many,' he groaned.

She gulped. 'We'll be working together—in here?'

'Mm,' he nodded. 'It's too cold now to work out in the garden, otherwise we could have gone outside.'

The idea of working in the confines of Jerome Towers' study, with the man himself, was totally unacceptable to her. She couldn't be in his company for two minutes without falling foul of his temper, or becoming angry herself, or, more dangerously, coming to realise how devastatingly attractive he was.

'In here?' she said again, stupidly.

'Yes.' He appeared to be becoming impatient. 'I got the idea from your brother. My original plan was for you to work full-time in the house, but when Brian told me you have training in shorthand and typing I came up with the idea of you helping me with my correspondence.'

'The training I did was at school, and that's——'

'So long ago,' Jerome taunted. 'Brian told me you're nineteen, so you left school three years ago. I doubt you've forgotten it in so short a time,' he derided.

'No, I haven't forgotten,' she agreed tightly.

'Then the matter is settled.' He moved back around the desk to sit down. 'You have until Monday to get used to the idea—I'll be in London until the weekend.'

'With Stella?' Megan couldn't resist taunting.

He frowned. 'What exactly did Roddy tell you about her?'

'Just that she's your woman,' Megan revealed disgustedly. 'And just as replaceable as all your other women have been.'

'Don't presume to judge my morals, Megan,' Jerome snapped. 'My relationships with the opposite sex last a hell of a lot longer than yours appear to.'

'A year isn't exactly a lifetime,' she scorned.

He scowled. 'My little brother seems to have told you

too damned much about my personal life!'

'Will that be all, Mr Towers?' she asked in a stilted voice. 'I have work to do.'

'That's all, for the moment. Your mother should be returning on Monday, if you could help Freda in the kitchen until then.'

'Oh yes, my mother. So nice of you to be concerned about her health,' she snapped. 'As long as she's back here waiting on you on Monday morning you couldn't give a damn about her.'

'Your mother is feeling a lot better today,' he informed her coldly. 'In fact she wanted to return to work tomorrow, but I told her to leave it until next week.'

'You *told* her?' Megan's eyes widened. 'Have you seen my mother today?'

'This morning,' he confirmed tightly.

'Oh.' She felt completely deflated by this information.

'I also went to see Patsy Jones. Apparently her husband has decided the work here is too much for her, that it's all got too much for her the last couple of months, and her doctor agrees with him. Donald says she's always been a nervy person, but that she's got worse lately.'

And being chased around the bedroom by Roddy Meyers was something the poor girl could well do without. Megan nodded. 'I remember her at school, she was nervy even then.'

'Mm. So you can see I'm not quite the ogre you like to think me. Be here at nine o'clock on Monday,' said Jerome tersely, dismissively.

Megan's mother felt well enough to sit up for a while that evening, and was still up when Brian came in for his evening meal.

'You're looking better.' He bent to kiss his mother on the cheek.

'I feel it,' she smiled up at him. 'What's this Megan's been telling me about your agreement with Mr Towers?'

Brian gave Megan a probing look, but could read nothing from her closed expression. 'Just let me wash,' he suggested, 'and we'll all talk about it.'

Megan had served up the chicken casserole and vegetables by the time he came back from having his wash, watching with satisfaction as her mother ate most of the small portion she had requested.

Again Brian eyed her. 'So Mr Towers spoke to you today,' he probed guardedly.

'Yes.' She began to eat her own meal.

'He mentioned it to me too,' their mother said thoughtfully. 'But the way I see it Megan has to be the one to decide what we do. She's the one who has to make the sacrifice. Working at The Towers isn't exactly what she had in mind for her career.'

'It won't be for ever, Mum,' Megan hastily reassured her.

'Does that mean you're agreeable?' Brian asked eagerly.

She shrugged. 'It's worth a try, I suppose.'

'That's great!' he enthused.

'But what happens if at the end of six months you have to sell to Mr Towers?' she asked him. 'Where are we going to live if we sell the farm?'

'Right here,' Brian told her happily. 'Mr Towers doesn't want the farm itself, only the land.'

'Okay,' she shrugged. 'But it's going to be the longest six months of my life. I just can't stand Jerome Towers!'

'He seemed to be under the impression that you're a friend of his brother.'

She gave Brian a sharp look. 'He told you that?'

'He just mentioned it. He said he thought the two of you had met at the hospital.'

'Yes, we did.' She pushed her plate away, her food only half eaten.

'He wasn't there when the scandal blew up, was he?' Brian said worriedly. 'That's all we need!' he groaned. 'Jerome Towers' brother a first-hand witness to your dismissal.'

Megan hoped Brian would never know just how much of a first-hand witness Roddy had really been; that could really blow his chances, because he would probably go out and beat the other man up. 'He'd already left before I did,' she said. Just!

'Then if he's a friend of yours you must invite him over for a meal,' her mother suggested.

'Oh—well, I'd rather not, Mum. Mr Towers doesn't approve of his brother going out with the hired help,' her mouth twisted bitterly.

'Megan!' Her mother scolded. 'Mr Towers simply isn't like that, he isn't in the least snobbish. Ask Mr Meyers over to tea on Sunday,' she encouraged.

'Not this week, Mum,' Megan evaded. 'We'll wait until you're completely better.'

'But I——'

'Not this week.' She stood up to kiss her mother affectionately on the cheek. 'Now back to bed with you, you've been up quite long enough for one day.'

When she came back from helping her mother into bed it was to find Brian waiting for her. 'I thought you would have gone over to Joyce's by now,' she frowned.

He looked up at her. 'I just wanted to make sure everything really was all right with you. You don't seem to like the idea of working for Jerome Towers. If you really couldn't stand it then we can just drop the idea.'

'Don't be silly,' she forced herself to smile. 'I've got

to work somewhere, and The Towers is as good a place as anywhere.'

'Sure?'

'Sure. I don't fancy getting up at the crack of dawn to dig potatoes anyway,' she grinned.

'Brussels, Megan,' he shook his head teasingly. 'We're into the sprout season now.'

'Oh.' She gave a rueful smile.

'A fine farmer you'd make!' her brother chuckled.

'Brian, what are you going to do if it doesn't work out?' she asked quietly.

He seemed unperturbed. 'Mr Towers says he has a job lined up for me on the estate.'

Megan's mouth tightened. 'He has it all worked out, doesn't he?'

Brian shrugged. 'He knows what he wants and tries to get it.' There was a wealth of respect in his voice.

'So I've noticed,' she said dryly. 'Are you sure you wouldn't rather just sell to him now? He seems pretty confident you're going to in the end anyway.'

'Maybe I am. But I owe it to Dad to give it another try. Six more months won't hurt us.'

'I suppose not.'

Megan wished she could really believe that. She tried to convince herself over the next few Jerome Towers-free days that the six months would soon pass, but she knew that to her it would be a lifetime. If only it could be as pleasant as these last few days without him had been—but she knew that as soon as he returned her resentment would return with him, and with it her knife-edged excitement in his presence.

She met her friend Tracy from the hospital on Saturday afternoon, and wandered around the shops in Redford with her. Poor Tracy, she was very upset when she realised that it was her information that had helped

Roddy Meyers find Megan's room that fateful night. Megan reassured her that he would have found her room some other way if Tracy hadn't told him, he had been that determined.

Paul called for her that evening, whistling appreciatively at her appearance. 'Surely all this isn't for the local hop?' he teased.

Megan looked down selfconsciously at the figure-hugging brown dress, the long length of her legs shown to advantage in the high-heeled sandals she wore. 'Have I gone over the top?' she asked uncertainly.

'Not as far as I'm concerned,' he grinned his appreciation, opening the door for her. 'Although you might shock a couple of the old biddies there.'

'That will please Mum no end,' Megan groaned. 'After the episode at the hospital she's extra-sensitive about my behaviour.'

At the last moment her mother had decided to go and visit her sister for the weekend. Her cold had almost gone, except for a slight cough that she couldn't seem to shake off. But she had only gone after warning Megan that she wasn't to mention what had happened at the hospital to anyone at the dance tonight. As if she would!

'You'll just raise a few eyebrows,' Paul assured her. 'The other men there will envy me.'

The hall was quite crowded by the time they arrived. Brian was already there with Joyce and her parents. Rachel Saunders was there too, with a stocky redhaired young man that Megan presumed to be Jeff Robbins. No wonder her mother had been surprised at her calling him good-looking; he looked pleasant enough, but he certainly wasn't handsome.

Megan and Paul collected a drink from the makeshift bar at the back of the room, then moved to circulate among their friends. Patsy and Donald Jones were there, Patsy's nervous beauty seeming to be more so than ever.

'I think this must be Roddy Meyers,' Paul suddenly muttered in her ear.

Megan spun round, groaning as she saw Roddy coming towards her. What on earth was he doing at a tame function like this? 'He's even worse than his brother!' she said furiously.

'Then he must be bad,' Paul said wryly, his challenging gaze fixed on the other man.

'Megan darling!' Roddy greeted warmly, making her cringe. 'How nice to see you here!'

'Is it?' she enquired tautly, sensing Paul's antagonism already.

'But of course,' Roddy smiled, completely unconcerned by her obvious anger. 'It's nice to see someone I know.' He looked at Paul. 'Aren't you going to introduce us, Megan?'

She did so, grudgingly.

Roddy held out his hand to the other man. 'So you're Paul,' he said consideringly.

Paul ignored the outstretched hand. 'Meyers,' he acknowledged tightly. 'Excuse us, Megan and I have to go and speak to some friends of ours,' implying that that was the last thing *he* was.

'But of course,' Roddy accepted smoothly, and his hand dropped to his side. 'I'll catch you later for a dance, Megan.'

'Over my dead body,' Paul muttered as they moved away. 'What a creep!'

Megan laughed at his expression. 'I did warn you.'

She studiously avoided Roddy for the rest of the evening, staying with her own crowd of friends, although she did notice him dancing with Patsy Jones a couple of times. Poor Patsy, she looked even more nervous than ever, shooting frightened glances at her husband as he watched them gloweringly. Donald had always been a possessive young man, and he obviously resented Roddy's interest in his wife.

Paul had gone over to the bar when Roddy came over for his dance, conveniently so, she thought. Roddy must have known by Paul's attitude towards him that he wouldn't welcome him even talking to her.

'No, thank you,' she politely refused his request.

'No?' He arched one blond eyebrow. 'Why not?'

'Because I don't like you,' she told him bluntly. 'I thought we'd agreed to stay out of each other's way?'

Roddy shrugged. 'It's only a dance, Megan.'

'Maybe later on,' again she refused.

'Now!' He pulled her determinedly on to the dance floor.

Without causing a scene Megan could do no other than dance with him, but she vowed to hate every minute of it. But Roddy was a good dancer, moving to the fast rhythm with an abandon that was catching. Some people actually stopped dancing to watch the uninhibited display they were putting on, others just gave them knowing looks as they themselves continued to dance.

Megan could see Paul's angry face as he stood on the edge of the crowd watching them, but she couldn't stop her own enjoyment of the music. Her body swayed and beckoned, her expression one of rapt enjoyment. Paul was great fun to be with, but he had absolutely no rhythm when it came to dancing, so it was good to be with someone who had a feel for the music and who wasn't ashamed to give in to it.

'Don't look now,' Roddy grinned at her, not even breathing heavily, 'but Big Brother is watching us!'

Megan seemed to come out of her trance, turning

almost guiltily to see Jerome Towers looking at them
with contempt. And standing at his side was the most
exquisitely beautiful woman Megan had ever seen. The
face was perfect, the figure delectable enough for any
man, and seeing the 'bright red hair', Megan presumed
this to be Stella, Jerome Towers' woman.

'Oh God!' she groaned, thankfully escaping as the
music came to an end.

She ran outside, aware of all the knowing looks being
thrown in her direction. And she had promised her
mother she would stay quietly in the background! The
locals would remember her behaviour this evening for a
long time to come.

And why had Jerome Towers had to be here! He
hadn't been in the hall when Roddy asked her to dance,
of that she was certain. He must have returned from
London today, bringing his beautiful mistress with him.

'Megan? Megan!' She could hear Paul calling for her
and she ducked behind the building, not up to facing
him yet, not up to facing anyone.

She could see him looking for her with a puzzled
frown on his face, finally giving up the search to go
back inside. Megan froze on the spot as she heard the
muted conversation of another couple, the hedgerow she
was standing behind hiding them from her view as much
as she was hidden from theirs. And yet she knew who
they were, knew and was shocked to the core.

'I don't like you being with her,' came the petulantly
female voice—Patsy Jones' voice!

'Don't you like her?' taunted the male voice—Roddy
Meyers' voice!

'I like Megan well enough,' Patsy dismissed. 'But
you love me, Roddy. You said you did,' she added uncertainly.

'And I do,' he soothed. 'But fiery Megan Finch is

providing a very good camouflage for us.' There was amusement in his voice. 'We don't want anyone to find out about us, so it's better if everyone thinks that Megan and I have something going for us. Can't you see that?'

'I suppose so. But—Roddy!' she groaned, cut off in mid-sentence. 'Oh, Roddy!' she sighed.

By peering around the hedge Megan could see the other couple locked together in a passionate kiss. Patsy and Roddy! Megan felt sick. How could Patsy do it? She had barely been married six months, surely not long enough for her to have tired of her husband and gone in search of another man. And what a man——! Roddy Meyers was the most selfish, egotistical individual she had ever met. And now it appeared he wasn't averse to breaking up marriages either.

'Well, well, well,' drawled a familiar voice, 'if it isn't my little secretary/housemaid!'

Megan spun round to face Jerome Towers, blushing fiercely at the contempt he made no effort to hide. She had to get him away from here, she couldn't let him see the other couple. Not that she was worried about Roddy, she couldn't give a damn about him, but until she had had a chance to talk to Patsy she would prefer that no one else knew of her affair. Just knowing that she knew about it could be enough to make Patsy stop seeing Roddy.

No wonder Patsy's nerves had got worse the last few months! Donald would go berserk if he knew his bride of only six months was having an affair with another man. Maybe he already suspected something; why else would he make Patsy leave The Towers?

'Good evening, Mr Towers,' she greeted stiffly. Oh dear, he was walking towards her! She was galvanised into action, stepping forward, a glowing smile to her lips. 'Would you care to dance, Mr Towers?' she invited.

Brown eyes narrowed, eyes the same colour brown as the velvet jacket he wore, the cream silk shirt contrasting perfectly, the dark brown trousers moulded to his long legs. He raised one dark eyebrow. 'Isn't it the prerogative of the male to ask that?'

Megan forced the smile to remain on her lips, although in reality she longed to wipe the sneer off his face. 'Never heard of equality, Mr Towers?' she enquired lightly.

'I've heard of it.' The disgust on his face showed his opinion of it, 'And I'll forgo the—pleasure of dancing with you, if you don't mind. I have a guest waiting for me inside.'

'Ah yes—Stella.'

'How did you know that?'

'Because she's a "beautiful little thing, with red hair".' Megan felt able to taunt him now, as a hurried look behind her had shown her that the other couple had gone. Thank goodness for that! How could Patsy be so stupid as to behave in that way at a function like this, when anyone might have seen her with Roddy? 'My mother's description,' she explained at Jerome Towers' questioning look.

'And yours?'

Megan shrugged. 'She's beautiful, and has red hair, what more can I say?'

'What more indeed? If you'll excuse me,' he nodded dismissively, 'I only came out to get Stella's wrap. She's feeling the cold.'

'Couldn't you think of some other way to warm her?' Megan scorned.

He eyed her coldly. 'We don't all have your desire for exhibitionism. I'm sure you and Roddy are just longing for me to get away so that you can finish what you started on that dance floor, so I won't keep you any longer.' He walked away.

Suddenly it was imperative that he shouldn't believe such things of her. 'Mr Towers!' she called. 'Please——'

'Yes?' he said harshly, not even bothering to turn and look at her.

'I—Oh, nothing,' she said dejectedly.

Jerome turned, his expression remote. 'I meant what I said about you and Roddy. I want no affair going on in my home.'

'There won't be——'

'Like hell there won't!' He was suddenly fierce, his expression savage. 'If I should catch you just once—I'd make your life hell, Miss Finch.'

'Haven't you done that already?' she asked dully. 'I can imagine nothing worse than having to work for you.'

'Oh, but there are, much worse things. As you'll find out if you cross me,' he warned before leaving.

Paul was furious with her when she got back into the hall, and suggested they leave immediately.

'I'm sorry,' Megan mumbled, Paul not having spoken a word during the journey.

'For what?' he rapped out.

She sighed. 'You know what.'

'You made a damned fool out of me,' he said angrily. 'What does Meyers mean to you?'

Megan looked startled. 'He doesn't mean anything to me. I hardly know the man.' And what she did know she didn't like!

'That wasn't the impression I got,' Paul scowled.

'He was a good dancer, Paul, that's all.'

'Dancing? That wasn't dancing!' he dismissed. 'That was——'

'All right,' she cut in, 'I know what it was. Maybe I

got carried away by the music, but——'

'Carried away!' he muttered disgustedly. 'It was obscene!'

'Paul——'

'I felt so damned stupid,' he burst out angrily, the car now parked in front of Megan's home. 'You went there with me, but you acted as if you were with *him*!'

'Please, Paul,' she put her hand on his. 'I've said I'm sorry. Would you like to come in for coffee?'

'No——'

'We'll be alone,' she enticed. 'Mum's away and Brian isn't home yet.'

'Well—okay,' he relaxed slightly. 'You've persuaded me.' He gave a rueful smile.

Several long minutes later Paul was feeling more amenable, his male pride back intact. They were sitting close together in one of the armchairs, Megan's mouth completely bare of lipstick, her hair in tangled disorder.

'Now I know you're my girl,' Paul sighed his satisfaction.

'Did you ever doubt it?' She snuggled against him, glad to be back on good terms with him.

'For a while tonight I did.' He bent to kiss her again. 'Oh hell!' he swore as a car drew up outside the house. 'That will be Brian.'

Megan looked at her wrist-watch and struggled to her feet. 'He's a bit early.' She grimaced. 'He's probably come home to tell me off.'

'Probably.' Paul ran a hand through his tousled hair.

She sighed, and went to open the door. Jerome Towers stood on the doorstep, tall and dark, and in a way, frightening. At once she was on the defensive. 'Yes?' she asked coldly, still raw from their last encounter.

'I didn't realise you were home, the house was in

darkness.' His gaze ran over her with slow appraisal, noting her lipstick-free mouth and untidy hair, Megan felt sure. 'I just called to see how your mother was.'

'She's a lot better, thank you,' she held the door halfway closed. 'She's away for the weekend.'

'I see. In that case——'

'Megan, is everything—Oh.' Paul came to stand behind her, looking just as dishevelled as she did. 'Good evening, Mr Towers,' he greeted politely.

Jerome Towers' mouth tightened as he looked at the two of them. 'Carter,' he returned curtly. 'I'm sorry I—interrupted you,' he spoke to Megan.

'I—Yes. I—I'll tell my mother you called,' she said awkwardly, well aware of the conclusions he had come to about this situation.

'Fine.' He nodded abruptly. 'Goodnight.'

They both echoed the word. Megan caught sight of the beautiful Stella as Jerome Towers opened his car door and the automatic light came on. She slowly closed the back door.

Paul grimaced. 'I can guess what he thought.'

So could Megan—and she didn't like it!

CHAPTER FIVE

MEGAN waited nervously in Jerome Towers' study on Monday morning, dreading his arrival. She had no idea how he was going to treat her, although after the fiasco of Saturday evening she could take a good guess.

Brian had been as furious with her as Paul had been, more so, and had given her a good talking to when he got home that evening. She had been suitably chastened all weekend, although Brian had very wisely not mentioned anything about it to their mother.

Megan had seen Jerome Towers once more since Saturday, had received a distant nod from him as he and the beautiful Stella had driven past her in his Jaguar as she walked down to see Wendy. Stella had looked more beautiful than ever, and Megan had wondered if it could be due to a night of love in her lover's arms.

She started visibly as he came into the room, flushing almost guiltily as he gave her a cursory glance before seating himself behind the desk. He had a pile of letters in his hand, and he put these down on the desk in front of him.

Suddenly he looked up. 'I won't ask if you had a nice weekend, the usual polite Monday morning greeting,' he mocked. 'From all accounts you had a pretty—hectic time.'

Megan frowned. 'I don't——'

'I think we'll forget about the weekend,' he interrupted tersely. 'It's best forgotten, wouldn't you say?'

'Yes.' She couldn't even meet his gaze.

'Then we'll forget about it,' he said briskly. 'Let's deal with this mail first.'

They worked steadily for the next hour, and Megan had a pile of letters to type replies to by the time all the envelopes had been opened. She hadn't realised there was quite so much paperwork involved in the running of an estate this size, although Jerome seemed to have his finger firmly on the pulse.

Finally he sat back, throwing some unwanted advertisements into the bin. 'Now we have to deal with my social commitments,' he sighed.

Megan frowned her puzzlement. 'Surely they aren't anything to do with me?' Remembering his beautiful mistress she thought his social life was strictly his own affair.

'This one is,' he picked up a letter that he had put aside earlier. 'Apparently I'm supposed to give a party at Christmas for all the local children.'

'Oh yes.' She remembered attending them herself, remembered that no matter how hard up old Squire Towers had been he had always put the annual Christmas party on for the children. 'You have to be Father Christmas,' she told Jerome absently, back in the time of roast turkey, jelly and icecream.

Jerome looked taken aback. 'I beg your pardon?'

Megan laughed, having relaxed with him in the last hour of working together. 'Father Christmas,' she grinned. 'Old Squire Towers always played him himself.'

He groaned. '*I'll* have to do that?'

'Well, it's up to you, of course, but it is expected.'

He grimaced. 'Then I suppose I'll have to do it. Could you go and get us some coffee while I get over the shock, and then you can tell me what else I'm supposed to do at this party.'

' 'Morning, love,' Freda greeted her cheerfully. 'Your mum's up with Mrs Reece cleaning the bedrooms,' and she carried on rolling out her pastry.

'Actually I've come to make coffee for Mr Towers and myself,' Megan told the cook, putting the necessary things on the tray.

'How are you getting on?' Freda asked interestedly.

'Oh, fine.' And strangely enough she was. Jerome seemed to have forgotten his anger with her, had forgotten it as he had suggested they forget her behaviour over the weekend. 'Does Mr Towers take sugar in his coffee?' She hesitated about adding the sugar-bowl, taking no sweetening herself.

'No.'

She didn't think he would. It was just her luck to meet Roddy outside the study, a Roddy she now regarded with open hostility.

'And how is my beautiful dancing partner this morning?' he mocked.

'I don't know,' she retorted. 'How is she?'

His look sharpened. 'What do you mean?'

Megan's eyes were green shafts of accusation. 'You know what I mean—Patsy Jones.'

He looked unperturbed. 'So you know about her and me.'

'Yes!' she snapped. 'You should be ashamed of yourself. She's a married woman, and you——'

The door behind them swung open, and Megan almost cringed as she met Jerome Towers' steely gaze. 'I thought I heard the two of you out here,' he said almost resignedly.

'Just saying good morning,' Roddy grinned at him.

Jerome took the tray out of Megan's trembling hands. 'Well, go and do it somewhere more private.'

Stella came out of the study behind Jerome, dramatically beautiful in black fitted blouse and snug-fitting black trousers. 'Ah, coffee,' she gave a dazzling smile. 'Lovely! Thank you, Miss—Rome, you haven't introduced us.' Her voice was low and sexy, her manner friendly and open.

This woman called him Rome! Megan felt an emotion rip through her that she didn't recognise. Then it was gone, and she felt only resentment that *her* cup of coffee had been claimed by the other woman.

'This is Megan Finch, Stella,' Jerome introduced curtly. 'My new secretary. Megan, Stella Mitchell.'

'Miss Mitchell,' Megan acknowledged shortly.

'Oh, please call me Stella,' the other woman invited warmly. 'I remember now, you were at the dance on Saturday.'

'Yes.' Megan studiously avoided looking at Jerome.

'It was fun, wasn't it?' Stella Mitchell smiled.

Megan searched the beautiful face for some sign of sarcasm, and found none. 'I'm sure you're used to more sophisticated entertainment,' she said sharply.

'Mm, I suppose London has more to offer in that direction.' Stella put her arm through the crook of Jerome's. 'But Jerome is in Norfolk,' she smiled happily up at her lover.

'Shall we have our coffee before it gets cold?' he suggested. 'Could you bring some sugar in to us, Miss Finch? It seems to have been omitted from the tray.'

'Oh, but you don't—Miss Mitchell takes sugar,' she realised dully.

'I have a sweet tooth,' the other woman admitted with a smile.

'You don't look as if you have,' Megan muttered, hoping that by the time she reached thirty she too had such a fantastic figure. Not that there was much chance of that, hers wasn't that good now.

Stella gave a happy laugh. 'I'm going to like you, Miss Finch.'

'I'll go and get the sugar,' Megan mumbled.

'I'll wait for you in the lounge,' Roddy told her.

Her expression hardened as she looked at him. 'Yes,' she agreed tightly.

Freda gave her a frowning look as she collected the discarded sugar-bowl. Megan just shrugged, hurrying back to the study.

'Thank you, Miss Finch,' Jerome said abruptly. 'Be back in fifteen minutes,' he added harshly.

'Nice to have met you, Megan.' Stella Mitchell sat on the arm of Jerome's chair, her arm across his shoulders, her fingers entangled in the dark hair at his nape.

Megan made a hasty escape from the sight of those rose-tinted nails caressing Jerome's firm flesh, finding she didn't like it at all.

Why didn't she like it? The answer didn't bear thinking about. Was she *falling in love* with Jerome Towers? She couldn't be, she just couldn't be!

'Megan!'

She looked up, startled, to see Roddy watching her impatiently from the lounge doorway. 'Sorry,' she mentally shook herself, 'I was miles away,' she excused.

His mouth twisted. 'So I gathered. Come in here.'

She went, shutting the door firmly behind her. 'It has to stop, Roddy,' she came straight to the point. 'If Donald should find out . . .'

'How did *you* find out?'

'I saw you together on Saturday evening, outside the hall.'

He sighed. 'I warned her about talking to me alone. She wasn't going to the dance to start with, and then when I got there I found her there with Donald.'

'Why not? He is her husband.'

Roddy raised his eyebrows. 'Is he?'

Megan frowned. 'What do you mean?'

He turned away. 'Nothing. It isn't important.'

'But it is,' she insisted. 'What did you mean by that remark?'

'It isn't my problem, it's Patsy's. If you want to know about her marriage you'll have to ask her. Personally, I don't consider it any of your business, not unless you're jealous?' He gave her a searching look.

'Jealous?' she scorned. 'I'm not jealous, I just don't like being used to cover up this affair.'

'And who's using you?' he asked calmly.

'You are. I heard you, Roddy. And I won't be used in that way. I won't help you shield your affair with Patsy. You'll have to find some other way to do it. A better idea would be to stop the affair, then you would have nothing to hide.'

'If I stop seeing Patsy will you come out with me instead?'

'No!'

'Then things stay as they are.'

'God, you sicken me. She's a married woman!' Her mouth tightened with determination. 'If you don't stop seeing her I'll tell your brother,' she threatened.

He looked unperturbed. 'And if you do that I'll tell him how you were dismissed from the hospital.'

'Because of you,' Megan said bitterly. 'Only because of you.'

'Jerome would find that even more unpalatable. He fancies you, you know,' Roddy told her harshly. 'He gets as mad as hell whenever any other male goes near you.'

Megan flushed. 'Don't be ridiculous! Your brother despises me, and most of that's your fault too.'

'You like him too!' he accused. 'Well, you've lost out there, Megan. I may not be averse to picking up his cast-offs, but he would never pick up mine.'

Her face showed her disgust. 'I'm not surprised!' Her look was scathing.

His face darkened angrily. 'You think you're such a clever little bitch, don't you?' he snarled. 'Well, you'll soon find that I make a much better friend than I do an enemy!'

Megan couldn't stop the shiver that ran down her spine. She had the feeling that Roddy Meyers could be a very dangerous person to anger—and there could be no doubt she had angered him. 'You don't scare me.' she said bravely. 'I just want this affair with Patsy Jones stopped.'

'And I've told you it's none of your damned business!' he shouted back.

The door swung open with a crash, and Jerome stood

angrily in the doorway, his fierce gaze running over both of them. 'What the hell is going on in here?' He strode furiously into the room. 'Your voices can be heard all over the house! Roddy,' he pinpointed his brother with glacial eyes, 'what's going on?'

'Just a slight disagreement,' his brother muttered.

Jerome sighed. 'Miss Finch?'

She blushed guiltily. 'I—we—your brother——'

'Just a lovers' quarrel, Rome,' Roddy cut in, moving to put his arm about Megan's shoulders. 'Calm down, darling,' he said as she began to struggle, his fingers biting painfully into her flesh. 'Megan's upset because I paid Patsy Jones a little attention on Saturday evening,' he explained.

She gasped. 'I——'

Jerome's gaze was scathing. 'Patsy is a married woman, Miss Finch, and hardly a likely candidate for your jealousy. Now could we get back to work?' he said sarcastically. 'And you, Roddy, get lost. I've warned Miss Finch about the two of you getting together in my time, and now I'll warn you—any more of this and you can go back to London.'

'But my operation——'

'Doesn't seem to have hindered any of your—activities,' Jerome drawled. 'If you wouldn't mind, Miss Finch?' he added with exaggerated politeness, opening the door for her to leave.

She could feel his disapproving gaze on the back of her neck as she walked ahead of him to the study, glad to see that Stella Mitchell was no longer there. Her humiliation would have been complete if the other woman had witnessed her chastisement. She stood awkwardly in the middle of the room, waiting for her employer's reprimand.

He sat at his desk, making a pyramid out of his

fingers, studying them intently. 'I hope there isn't going to be a repetition of this every day,' he looked up harshly.

'But——'

'Let me finish, Miss Finch,' he snapped coldly. 'I've warned you repeatedly about your behaviour with my brother. I will not have it, do you understand!'

'But——'

'Does Roddy know about Carter?' he bit out.

Megan looked bewildered. 'Paul? But he——'

'Does Carter know about Roddy?' he didn't allow her to finish.

'No!' she shuddered.

'My God!' Jerome stood up to angrily pace the room, stopping in front of her to look her critically up and down. 'What is it about you? We're like bees around a honeypot——'

'We?' she cut in dazedly.

'Yes, *we*!' He pulled her roughly towards him. 'All the available men in the area seem to find you fascinating, including me. You must be good, very good,' he murmured, his warm, caressing gaze fixed on her parted lips. 'Maybe I should find out how good.'

'Mr Towers!' Megan was shocked, frightened too.

'Rome,' he invited softly, his head slowly lowering. 'Call me Rome,' his mouth finally claimed hers.

As soon as his lips parted hers Megan knew she had been waiting for this, had craved his kisses ever since that first day when he had brought Bertha back to the farm, had wanted this fierce passion even then, although his gentleness at the time had moved her.

Their desire for each other was like a vulcano erupting, Megan shuddering as she felt the strength of his thighs pressed against her. Those hands she had so admired now ran slowly from her hip to her breast, lingering there, releasing the top button of her blouse before he lowered his head to move his warm lips across her sensitive flesh.

He undid another button to her blouse, and another, and another, until he could put his hands inside and cup her breasts. But even then he wasn't satisfied, and one hand moved to her back to swiftly dispense with the single fastening to her bra.

To Megan all this seemed to be happening in a dream. It was as if she stood outside herself, looking down at the two of them as Jerome leant back against the desk, pulling her close to him, his dark head lowering to capture the rosy tip of one creamy breast between his lips, nibbling gently on the throbbing flesh.

But the feelings he aroused weren't a dream, nor the pleasure that shot through every particle of her body, or the way her legs suddenly seemed to buckle beneath her, causing him to pull her even closer to his own body. God, she thought, if she died at this moment she wouldn't care!

He raised his head. 'Well?' he asked softly.

'Oh, Rome!' she sighed, utterly lost in her passion for this man.

Suddenly he thrust her away from him, buttoning his shirt where seconds earlier she had feverishly undone it. His lip curled back. 'Now I know why all the men in the area want you,' he scorned harshly.

Megan blinked dazedly, feeling bereft without his arms about her. 'You do?'

'Oh yes,' he let his gaze slowly roam over her. 'You're so damned easy they're all queueing up to get into bed with you!'

She swallowed hard, feeling sick. 'Wh—What did you say?'

He gave a harsh laugh. 'I think you heard me. Do up

your blouse, Megan, you look like the wanton you are standing there like that.'

She became aware of her nakedness, and her face turned fiery red as she tried to refasten her bra. It wasn't easy, and finally Jerome pushed her hands away, pulling back her blouse and doing up the catch to her bra himself. Megan was stunned by his coolness after what she had thought to be shared passion.

'Why did you do that?' she asked jerkily. 'Why did you kiss me?'

'Why not?' he shrugged. 'Everyone else seems to be doing it. Now about this party . . .'

'Party?' Megan frowned. 'What party?'

'The Christmas party for the children,' he explained patiently. 'Will you know how to organise it?'

She blinked to clear her head. How could he stand there and calmly discuss a children's party when she felt completely dazed? He was unmoved by the passionate scene that had just taken place in this room, had been through the same thing with hundreds of other women, whereas for her it had been the first time she had experienced sexual tension, the first time she had known that rise of desire, that longing for the wonderful release she knew came with full lovemaking.

And Jerome was accusing her of being a wanton! Maybe she hadn't acted like the amateur she was, feeling an instinctive urge to touch him, to caress and kiss him as intimately as he had her. But she was an amateur, a complete innocent when it came to lovemaking, although she knew it would only take one touch of those experienced hands to bring her to fever pitch once again.

'Rome——,' she flinched at his anger. 'Jerome—er—Mr Towers, I——'

'Will you do up your blouse, for God's sake!' he rasped. 'Or do you want me to do that too?'

'I—No!' Her hands moved automatically to do up the buttons. 'Just now——'

'Was an experiment, Megan.' He moved around the desk to once more sit down. 'You really like it, don't you,' he said insultingly. 'You get turned on even by men you don't particularly like.'

Her eyes darkened with pain. 'No . . .' she shook her head.

'Yes!' he insisted. 'I've heard about girls like you, but I've never met one before. You like sex so much, enjoy it so much, that the identity of your partner doesn't really matter to you. All you require from him is that he be male and know how to treat you in bed.'

Megan's hand swung up and caught him on the side of his face. She hit him with all the strength that was in her, not sparing another glance in his direction as she left the room, her head held high.

'Come back for your own coffee, love?' Freda smiled at her. 'My, you do look pale! Sit down and I'll bring your coffee over to you.' She sat down opposite Megan at the kitchen table. 'Been working you hard, has he?'

Megan felt numb. Jerome Towers had meant to humiliate her, sexually humiliate her, and he had succeeded. Too well! She felt as if she never wanted another man to touch her. She felt dirty and degraded, most of all degraded. Her experiences with the men in this family were enough to put her off males for life. And she wasn't sure it hadn't!

'You do look ill,' Freda frowned her concern. 'Maybe you should go home.'

'No!' She wouldn't give Jerome that satisfaction. 'I'll be fine.' She had her father's dogged personality, and neither of them had been known to run away from a fight. 'There, I feel better now,' she smiled brightly.

'Sure? You still look pale, and——'

'I'll be fine, Freda—really. I just needed my coffee.'

'Did Miss Mitchell take yours?'

'Mm,' she admitted ruefully. 'Well, I'd better get back to work now.'

She hesitated outside the study door, finally bracing her shoulders before taking a firm hold of the door-handle and going inside. Jerome Towers slowly raised his head, watching her as she picked up her notepad before going over to the desk in front of the window. Megan didn't say a word but began typing the replies he had dictated to her earlier.

'Miss Finch,' he finally rapped out.

She stopped typing. 'Mr Towers?' she raised one eye-brow questioningly.

He stood up. 'The next time you come into this room, knock first!' He slammed out of the study.

Megan was lucky enough to meet Patsy Jones that evening as the two of them came out of the small local grocery store.

'Patsy!' she halted the other girl as she would have walked away. 'I was hoping I'd see you. Do you have time to talk?'

Patsy looked up at her with apprehensive eyes. 'What do we have to talk about?'

Megan sighed. 'I'm sure Roddy has told you.'

Blue eyes flashed. 'Rod—er—Mr Meyers?' Patsy amended quickly. 'What does he have to do with us talking?'

'He hasn't told you, has he?'

Patsy frowned. 'Told me what?'

'That I know about the two of you. Are you mad, Patsy?' Megan exclaimed in exasperation. 'Don't you realise all that you risk losing for that worthless——'

'You're just jealous!' the other girl cut in angrily.

'Roddy told me about you, about the way you keep chasing him, even at the hospital. But he doesn't want you,' pansy-blue eyes blazed. 'He wants *me*!'

'I don't want him,' Megan dismissed disgustedly. 'I think he's the biggest creep I've ever met. And if you're fooled by——'

'Shut up!' Patsy said forcefully. 'Just shut up. You're like all the rest, always trying to tell me what to do. I'll see Roddy as much as I want to, so just leave me alone!' She walked hurriedly away.

'Patsy . . .'

She turned, her expression fierce. 'Just leave me alone, will you!'

Megan shrugged defeat, then walked slowly home. If Patsy didn't want to be helped then she didn't see what she could do about it. But it was such a shame. She knew that to Roddy it was all a game, the fact that Patsy was married had probably just made the chase more interesting. Unfortunately Roddy was one of those men who enjoyed the chase more than the capture, and Megan didn't think it would take him long to tire of the sweet, unsophisticated Patsy.

'Did you get the bread, love?' her mother came through from the kitchen as she let herself into the house.

'Mm.' Megan handed it over.

'I've asked Paul to stay to supper,' her mother told her.

'That will be nice,' she replied absently

Her mother frowned at her lack of enthusiasm. 'I thought so. How did your day go?'

Megan managed a casual shrug, although her body ached with the tension of trying to act normally all day, especially when all she had really wanted to do had been to run away and hide. After he had slammed out of the study Megan had only seen Jerome once more, and that had been when he had driven off some time during the afternoon with the beautiful Stella.

She had discovered by helping Mrs Reece around the house in the afternoon that Jerome and his mistress had bedrooms facing each other across the corridor. It didn't need superhuman intelligence to work out that only one of these bedrooms would be occupied at night.

'Did you hate it?' Her mother looked worried.

'It was no worse than I thought it would be,' Megan evaded. 'What time will the boys be in to supper?' she changed the subject.

'Any time now. I'd better get back in the kitchen and see to the sprouts.'

Megan followed her, sniffing appreciatively. 'Smells nice. What is it?'

'Roast chicken.' Her mother smiled. 'Your father's favourite.'

Megan's face darkened with concern. 'You still miss him, don't you?'

'Well, of course I do,' her mother nodded. 'Some marriages become stale, a case of taking each other for granted, but that never happened to us. We were happy together, and we always said we would like that sort of marriage for you.'

'I've yet to meet the right man, Mum,' Megan said regretfully.

'I thought Paul . . .'

Megan slowly shook her head. 'He's a very good friend, and I enjoy being with him, but—well, there's something missing from the relationship.' Sexual excitement was what was missing, she knew that! After this morning in Jerome's arms she knew she could never marry Paul, not in all honesty. He had never induced that volcanic excitement in her, never made her feel so—

VISIT 4 MAGIC PLACES FREE

PORTUGAL

SWEET REVENGE by Anne Mather
When Antonia innocently became part of an
attempted swindle, Raoul planned to carry
out his "sweet revenge." She fled from his
exquisite castle in Portugal, but Raoul, used
to having his way with women, found her.

TEXAS

NO QUARTER ASKED by Janet Dailey
All Stacy had been looking for was a place to
sort things out for herself. But the beautiful
invalid had not reckoned on the ruggedly
handsome Cord Harris, powerful Texan
cattle baron.

CYPRUS

GATES OF STEEL by Anne Hampson
Disenchanted with love, Helen fled to exotic
Cyprus, only to encounter the handsome,
arrogant Leon Petrou. His proposal of marriage
surprised Helen, but she accepted. It would be
solely a marriage of convenience, she thought.
But Helen was wrong.

FRANCE

DEVIL IN A SILVER ROOM by Violet Winspear
Paul Cassailis, master of the remote French
chateau of Satancourt, desired the quiet,
reserved Margo. But love had brought Margo
pain once before. Now Paul stood accused of
murder. And Margo discovered to her horror that
she loved him.

Love surrounds you in the pages of Harlequin romances

Harlequin Presents romance novels are the ultimate in romantic fiction... the kind of stories that you can't put down... that take you to romantic places in search of adventure and intrigue. They are stories full of the emotions of love... full of the hidden turmoil beneath even the most innocent-seeming relationships. Desperate clinging love, emotional conflict, bold lovers, destructive jealousies and romantic imprisonment—you'll find it all in the passionate pages of **Harlequin Presents** romance novels.

Let your imagination roam to the far ends of the earth. Meet true-to-life people. Become intimate with those who live larger than life.

Harlequin Presents romance novels are the kind of books you just can't put down... the kind of experiences that remain in your dreams long after you've read about them.

TAKE THESE **4** BEST-SELLING
HARLEQUIN ROMANCES

FREE SEE EXCITING DETAILS INSIDE

Canada Post
021
Postes
Canada

so alive and *wanting*. She had wanted Jerome this morning, and he had wanted her, no matter how cruelly he had rejected her.

'Paul's serious about you,' her mother told her. 'Let him down gently, Megan love.'

The opportunity to do that came sooner than she had expected, that evening to be precise. Brian had gone to Joyce's, her mother had gone to visit one of her friends in the village, and Paul came back to keep Megan company after having been home to change.

'This is cosy.' He had his arm about her shoulders, pulling her close.

They were seated on the sofa in the lounge, a cheery fire in the hearth, the television turned down low. It was the sort of situation Megan had been hoping to avoid; her emotions were all confused after this morning. She felt sure Jerome wouldn't feel the same reluctance to make love to his mistress.

She took a deep breath. 'Paul——'

'Mm,' he nuzzled into her throat. 'You taste good,' and he gently nibbled her skin.

'Paul!' she wriggled away from him.

He looked hurt. 'What's wrong, love? You don't seem yourself this evening.'

Probably because she didn't feel herself! She kept wondering what Jerome was doing, who he was with—and if it was the beautiful Stella, if he was making love to her. It was like a knife twisting in her throat to think of the other woman being the recipient of those caressingly knowledgeable hands, making Megan wonder again at the depth of her own feelings for Jerome Towers.

'Megan?' Paul was frowning down at her.

'Sorry,' she brought herself back from her disturbing thoughts. 'I'm just feeling tired, I think.'

'But I thought you said your first day hadn't been too difficult.'

'I said it hadn't been hard work,' she corrected. 'I wouldn't deny it's been difficult.'

'You still don't like Mr Towers?'

'I—I no longer *dis*like him.' She didn't feel she could tell an out-and-out lie. 'He—he works hard on the estate,' she rushed on. 'No one can deny that. I'm surprised he finds the time to deal with his other business interests.'

Paul nodded. 'He has a capacity for work that I've never seen equalled. He enjoys it, thrives on the challenge. He's the same with women, he always likes to win.'

Megan blushed, knowing first hand of Jerome Towers' need to conquer. 'You sound envious,' she teased to hide her pain.

'Not me,' he grinned. 'Although it would be nice to have that lethal charm of his.' He leant back, sighing his satisfaction. 'But I'd rather settle for spending the rest of my life with you.'

Her heart sank. 'Paul——'

'When shall we get married?' He didn't seem to have noticed her suddenly pale face. 'We have no reason to wait now that you aren't going to finish your training.'

'Paul!' This time it was a groan.

'Easter would be nice,' he mused. 'Don't you think so?' He looked down at her.

Megan bit her lip painfully. 'I don't remember you ever asking me to marry you,' she pointed out gently.

'No? Well——I——' he flushed a fiery red. 'You will, won't you?'

'I——' She was interrupted by a loud hammering on the front door. 'Who on earth can that be?' she frowned. 'It's after ten.'

Paul stood up. 'Better let me go, you shouldn't be answering the door to anyone at this time of night.'

Megan followed him out into the passageway, and her eyes widened as she saw Jerome Towers standing on the doorstep, a rather wet Jerome Towers as it was pouring down with rain.

'Come in,' she invited hurriedly. The furious anger in his eyes was ominous.

He grimaced, 'I'd better not. I'm dripping wet and I have mud all over my boots.'

'For goodness' sake come in,' she said impatiently, pulling him inside. He was so wet, water was dripping off him as he had said it was. 'What on earth possessed you to walk over here in this weather?' she frowned at him.

'Your damned cow *possessed* me,' he groaned angrily.

Megan looked startled. 'Bertha?'

'Do you have any other?' he queried sarcastically.

'Did she come over to The Towers again?' she asked with dread.

'How clever of you to guess! Yes, she came to The Towers, and she knocked one of my fences over in the process,' he scowled darkly.

'Is she outside?'

Jerome gave her a pitying look. 'Well, I hardly walked here without her.'

'I'll go and put her back in the shed,' Paul spoke for the first time, his hand resting on Megan's shoulder. 'All right, love?' he asked softly.

She looked up at him gratefully, glad he wasn't going to witness the scene Jerome Towers was obviously spoiling for. 'Thanks, Paul. You know where she goes?' His nod confirmed it, and she watched as he pulled on his coat and went out into the rain. 'Come into the lounge, Mr Towers,' she invited politely. 'It's warmer there.'

'My boots——'

'Take them off if you're that worried about them,' she said impatiently, going through to the lounge without him.

Seconds later he followed her, without the boots and soaking wet topcoat. He wore a black rollnecked sweater and black corduroys, the latter moulded to the long length of his thighs. His presence here when she had been thinking about him so deeply was very unnerving.

He went over to the fire, warming his hands in front of the blaze, the dark swathe of his hair falling forward over his forehead. Suddenly he turned to look at her. 'It can't continue, you know.'

'I'm sorry. You see, Bertha is probably looking for the rest of her herd. We sold them to you. I—I think she misses them.'

Jerome eyed her mockingly. 'She *misses* them?'

Megan flushed. 'Well, it's possible. She has feelings, you know.'

'I'm sure you know her well enough to realise what's wrong with her,' he taunted.

'There's no need to be sarcastic!' she flashed.

'I didn't know I was. And when I said it can't continue, I wasn't referring to Bertha's wanderings.'

Her chin went up in challenge. 'What, then?'

'I think you know what—this game of musical beds, you've been playing with my brother and Paul Carter. I sounded Roddy out this evening, and he obviously has no idea how far things have gone between you and your young friend Paul.'

Megan flushed with anger. 'My friendship with Paul is none of your brother's concern!'

'Not even when he's sleeping with you too?'

'He isn't!' she gasped.

Jerome shook his head, his expression one of disgust. 'You're going to get caught out, Megan. I don't know how you've managed to keep them apart so far. Roddy got home about an hour ago—what did you do, tell him you had a headache as a means of getting rid of him so that Carter could join you here?'

'I haven't seen Roddy this evening,' she denied heatedly. 'He's probably been with——'

'Yes?' he prompted sharply.

'He hasn't been with me,' she told him firmly. 'Ask Paul, we've been together all evening.'

His mouth twisted. 'I have no intention of asking Carter anything. I can imagine the construction he would put on my interest. I won't be another of your men, Megan, possibly the lunchtime session you first offered me.'

'You conceited swine! I offered to have lunch with you, not jump into bed with you.'

'One seems to lead to the other where you're concerned,' he said insultingly. 'I doubt Roddy will be hurt by your duplicity, but Carter might be. Why don't you finish with him and let him find himself some nice girl to marry?'

'He wants to marry *me*!' Megan told him defiantly.

Brown eyes narrowed, his look assessing. 'Has he asked you?'

'Yes,' she took pleasure in telling him.

'And your answer? No, don't bother to tell me,' he taunted. 'You aren't going to marry him. You would never be able to settle for one man.'

'I——' She longed to say that yes, she was going to marry Paul. But she couldn't use him in that way. She had no intention of marrying him, and he could only be hurt if she were to say she was. 'I'm not going to marry him,' she admitted tautly. 'But not for the reason you said.' Her eyes flashed deeply green.

'Time I was going.' He moved to pull on his coat and boots. 'Carter will never know what a lucky escape he's had,' he added scornfully.

'God, I hate you!' Her vehemence was unmistakable.

'No more than I hate you. But I want you too.' He made the admission as if it were forced out of him. 'You knew that this morning, didn't you? Of course you did,' he answered his own question. 'You know exactly how a man's body functions, know damn well what a turn-on those little animal moans of yours are. Well, I may not be a saint where women are concerned, but I try not to go in for used goods, especially when they've been used the amount of times you have. Oh no!' he stopped her hand as it swung up to hit him. 'You were lucky to get away with it the first time, don't push your luck.'

Paul came in just then, and so Megan swung away from Jerome. 'Is everything all right?' Her voice quivered, her nerves shot to pieces. Animal moans? Had she really done that?

'Fine. Let me drive you home, Mr Towers,' Paul offered instantly. 'It's still pouring down out there.'

Jerome straightened. 'I wouldn't want to drag you away from your—friend?'

Megan shot a sharp glance at Paul to see if he had noticed that hesitation, but he seemed not to have done. She looked resentfully at Jerome, hating the scorn she could see in his face. 'I wouldn't send a dog out on a night like this,' her insult was unmistakable. 'Of course Paul must drive you.'

She finally got them both out of the house, then hurried back inside, tears streaming down her face. She had just told the man she loved that she hated him, and that his hatred of her was genuine was obvious!

CHAPTER SIX

GOING in to work the next day took all Megan's willpower. How could she have let herself fall in love with Jerome Towers? She must be mad, mad! And the opinion he had of her——!

' 'Morning, beautiful,' Roddy swaggered into the study. 'I hear you had a word with Patsy yesterday.'

Jerome hadn't come in, otherwise, Megan had no doubt, Roddy wouldn't be so sure of himself. Jerome had a way of reducing him to the gauche young man he really was. 'I tried,' she said defensively

'Well, in future stay out of it,' he snapped. 'Patsy's old enough to make her own decisions.'

'The way I did?' she scorned. 'I didn't choose to have you invade my room at the hospital, I didn't choose to get sacked because of you either.'

'How you love to go on about that,' he scorned. 'For heaven's sake, it wasn't the end of the world.'

Megan went white. 'It was the end of my career! But you couldn't give a damn about that, could you?'

'Not particularly,' he shrugged. 'You don't seem to have had any difficulty finding yourself a job.' His eyes narrowed on her. 'Still got your crush on Rome?'

She flushed. 'I never had a crush on him!' Which was perfectly true. If it was merely a crush she felt for him she wouldn't feel so nervous for her own future, would know that sooner or later she would get over her feelings for him.

'Prove it,' Roddy challenged.

She frowned. 'How?'

103

'Quite easily.' He took a determined step towards her, pulling her hard against him and grinding his mouth down on hers before she had time to protest.

Nausea filled her throat and she struggled against him for all she was worth, finally kicking him hard on the shin, a gleam of satisfaction in her eyes as he leapt back with a cry of pain.

'You little bitch!' He raised his hand as if to hit her.

'Oh no, you don't!' Jerome arrested that hand before it made contact with her cheek. He pushed Roddy roughly away from Megan. 'What the hell do you think you're doing?' His eyes burnt like twin coals as he looked at his brother, a white ring of anger about his mouth.

'Megan was——'

'I'm not asking about Megan, I'm asking what you were doing!' His stance was challenging as he looked down at his young brother.

'We were having an argument,' Roddy told him resentfully.

Jerome's mouth twisted tauntingly. 'That much was obvious. Was this argument so serious that you had to hit her?'

'I didn't hit her!'

'You were damn well going to. Now why?'

Roddy looked sulky. 'She kicked me.'

'So I saw. I also saw *why* she kicked you. Oh, get out of here, Roddy. It's obvious I'm not going to get anything out of you.'

Once Roddy had reluctantly left them Megan sank faintly down into a chair, the nausea still with her.

'Put your head down,' a firm voice ordered, a hand resting gently at her nape as he assisted her. 'Right down,' Jerome encouraged.

After several minutes she felt able to sit upright,

though her head was still spinning slightly. 'I—I'll be all right now,' and she gave a wan smile.

'You're deathly white.' He came down on his haunches beside her. 'You really didn't like him kissing you, did you?' he said in a puzzled voice.

'I loathed it!' She swallowed down the rising nausea once again.

Jerome frowned. 'But I thought—You don't even like Roddy, do you?' he said with conviction.

'I hate him!'

He shook his head in confusion. 'Then why do you go out with him?'

'I told you I haven't been out with him, not ever.'

His frown deepened. 'Then if it isn't you who the hell *is* he seeing? Obviously someone he doesn't want me to know about.'

Megan stiffened; she did not want to involve Patsy. 'I wouldn't know.' She pushed back her long blonde hair.

His hand under her chin forced her to look at him. 'But you do know who his girl-friend is.' He was quick to notice the aversion of her eyes.

'I——'

'Don't deny it,' he advised softly. 'I can see you do know.'

'If you want to know any more about it you'll have to ask Roddy.'

'I intend to,' Jerome stated grimly. 'And I shall demand some answers. He deliberately led me to believe—I'm sorry,' his tone was rigid. 'It would seem I've misjudged you.'

Megan looked at him beneath lowered lashes. 'Only *seem*?'

He stiffened, towering over her with haughty resentment. 'I *have* misjudged you,' he corrected coldly. 'And Paul Carter?'

'A friend,' she answered without hesitation.

'But he would like to be more?'

She looked down at her hands. 'Yes.'

'But you aren't interested?'

'No.'

'And then there were none,' he mused. 'Interesting. Get your coat, Megan, we're going out,' he told her briskly.

'Out? But——'

'In the course of business, Megan,' he taunted her uncertainty. 'I may have eliminated the two men I thought were predominant in your life, but I'm not conceited enough to presume you would now be willing to go out with me. Besides——'

'Rome,' Stella Mitchell appeared in the doorway. 'Oops!' she gave a mischievous smile. 'Sorry, I forgot you'd be with your secretary. I came to take my morning coffee with you.'

Here was Jerome's 'besides'! Stella Mitchell was the woman in his life, and had been for the last year. Megan had no reason to suppose he would want to replace her, and even if he did Megan wasn't sure she wanted that sort of transient relationship with anyone.

Jerome's smile was warm as he looked at the other woman. 'Not this morning, Stella. Megan and I have to go out.' He pulled on his thick sheepskin jacket as if to prove the point.

'If you would rather Miss Mitchell went with you . . .' Megan said awkwardly.

His look was cold. 'I've already told you this is a business trip. While Stella may have many accomplishments, shorthand is not one of them.'

'Oh, I see, you want me to make notes,' Megan nodded her understanding.

'Why else did you think I was taking you?' he mocked,

turning his coat collar up to meet the cold weather outside.

She flushed and stood up. 'I'll just get my coat.'

'Right.' He turned to kiss Stella briefly on the mouth. 'See you later. I'll be waiting outside, Megan.' His voice hardened.

She collected her coat from the kitchen, hurrying through the spacious hallway because she didn't want to anger Jerome by keeping him waiting.

'You'll pay for that,' Roddy told her in a husky voice.

Megan spun round to see him standing at the top of the stairs, a shiver of fear running through her. And she was frightened of this man, had been terrified when he had raised his hand to hit her. Now she didn't say a word but just turned on her heel and ran, not caring that he was laughing at her.

Jerome was seated in a dark green Range Rover, waiting while she fastened her safety-belt before driving off.

'What happened to the Jaguar?' Megan opened the conversation; their silence was oppressive.

'Nothing happened to it.' He was a very careful driver, quick and precise, considerate of other motorists. 'A Range Rover is easier for driving around the estate, especially down muddy dirt-tracks.'

Her eyes were wide. 'I didn't realise we were going over the estate.'

'I have to check on fences. Bertha's accident yesterday reminded me I hadn't checked them over lately.'

Megan flushed at the mention of Bertha's accident. 'We'll pay you for the fence. Just send us the bill.'

'That won't be necessary,' he returned. 'The fence wasn't as badly damaged as I thought it was. A few nails and it was as good as new.'

'The nails——'

'Don't you dare offer to pay for them!' he ground out. 'Or I'll put you over my knee and spank you.'

'Ooh, nice!' Megan reacted as she would have done to one of her friends. 'Sorry,' she blushed. 'I meant——'

Jerome laughed, a genuinely amused laugh. 'I know what you meant. I was young once.'

'You still are! I mean——'

'Thank you,' he bowed, his eyes warm with laughter.

'I—er—Isn't it Jeff Robbins' job to check on damaged fences?' she asked to cover her embarrassment.

'It is,' he confirmed. 'But Jeff's leaving at the end of the month——'

'He is?'

'Mm. He was contracted for six months, and he's decided not to renew that contract. He and Rachel are getting married, you know, and as Rachel's father is retiring at the end of the year Jeff is going to run his farm for him.'

'And who is going to run your estate for you?'

'I am—until Brian takes over.'

Megan looked at him wide-eyed. '*That's* the job on the estate you have lined up for him?'

'Mm,' he nodded.

'Does he know?'

'No. And I don't want him told. He has to be given every chance to get your own farm back on its feet.'

'So that it's in good condition when you buy it?'

He quirked an eyebrow at her. 'Do you still believe that?'

'No,' she admitted huskily. 'You're really going to make Brian your new manager?'

'Yes. Hell, look at that fence!' After that he launched into a list of things he wanted done or changed, so that by lunchtime Megan had quite a long list of things in her notebook to be done.

'Lunch?' Jerome turned to smile at her.

She looked at her wrist-watch, surprised to see it was one o'clock. 'I am getting hungry,' she admitted.

'The Green Man?'

'Oh, I—I didn't expect you to provide me with a meal. I thought we were going back to The Towers.'

He quirked an eyebrow. 'You don't want to have lunch with me?'

'Yes. No! I—I'd like to,' she said shyly.

'Good.' His hand briefly touched hers. 'I'm sorry about yesterday,' he said huskily. 'About all of it.'

'I——'

'Don't say anything, Megan,' he told her with a sigh. 'Let's just have lunch. You never know,' he gave a slight smile, 'we might even end up by becoming friends.'

Friends! She didn't want to be his *friend*. She forced herself to smile back at him. 'We might,' she agreed lightly.

'But you doubt it,' he accepted dryly.

She *knew* it. She couldn't ever be friends with this man, she wanted him as a lover, not as a friend. But at least now he wasn't sniping at her all the time, insulting her at every turn. Lunch was pleasant, their conversation polite and impersonal. Megan thought that was maybe a good thing, at least that way they didn't argue.

'I have to call on the Joneses,' Jerome told her on the drive back. 'Tam Jones had a heart attack a few months ago and I usually call on him a couple of times a week to see how he is. Is that all right with you?'

'Yes, fine.' She frowned her bewilderment. 'You take

an extraordinary interest in the people around here, even more than old Squire Towers did.'

'You didn't expect me to?'

'Well . . . no,' she answered honestly.

'Disappointed?' he mocked.

'Pleasantly surprised.'

His mouth quirked. 'I'm sure you're disappointed,' he drawled. 'The first time we met you had this pre-conceived idea of what I was like.'

'When I thought you were Jeff Robbins,' she said with remembered resentment.

Jerome smiled. 'At least I found out what you thought of me. Who did you get that impression from?'

'I—Your uncle always said you were——'

'Ah,' he nodded. 'My uncle. Uncle Henry told you I was a pompous, arrogant snob, with ideas above my station.'

Megan almost gaped. 'You knew what he said about you?'

He laughed at her surprise. 'He felt no compunction about saying it to my face.'

'I see,' she bit her lip. 'Well, he did call you that, many times, but I don't remember him ever saying any-thing about being above your station. Why did he resent you so much?'

'Dislike, Megan,' Jerome corrected. 'My uncle disliked me intensely. He would have left The Towers to someone else if he could, but unfortunately for him the estate is entailed and always passes to the eldest male heir.'

'Why did he dislike you?' Her curiosity was fully aroused now.

'Does that mean you don't think I'm a pompous, arrogant snob?'

She blushed. 'You know I don't.'

'I *hope* you don't. My uncle disliked me because of who my mother was. Don't look like that, Megan!' he chuckled. 'She wasn't a murderess or anything like that, she just happened to be Italian.'

So that was where he got those gorgeous brown eyes from, and the slight darkness to his skin.

'Uncle Henry had a dread of "furriners",' Jerome mocked. 'Although strangely enough this dislike didn't apply to Roddy too,' he shrugged. 'Maybe because Roddy is so fair. Anyway, for whatever reason, he didn't like me. You know the state everything at The Towers was in when he died? Well, I'd offered to help him, after all it was my inheritance, but he turned me down. Do you know why?' he mused. 'Because it was my mother's money, left to me when she died. When my father married my mother Uncle Henry didn't speak to him ever again.'

Megan had been totally wrong about this man! She had taken other people's opinions of him and made them her own, without even giving him a chance to prove them wrong.

'You can wait here if you like.' Jerome climbed down from the Range Rover. 'I'll only be with Tam a few minutes.'

'How is he?' she asked.

'Angry with his own weakness.'

Remembering Tam Jones' explosive Welsh temper, Megan opted to stay in the Range Rover. Tam wouldn't be a man to have patience with his illness, and she didn't think he would welcome her seeing him like that. She spotted Donald in the backyard a few minutes after Jerome had left her and decided to go and have a chat with him. Maybe she would inadvertently find out what was wrong with his marriage to Patsy. Not that she thought he would turn around and tell her, he was as clam-like as his father, but he might let something slip without realising it.

'Hello, Donald,' she greeted brightly.

'Megan,' he nodded, continuing to load up the van with his building supplies. He and his father were in business together, taking care of all the small local jobs that needed doing. Maybe that was the trouble, maybe with his father ill he was having to take too much of the work on himself and was neglecting Patsy.

'Keeping busy?' she probed.

'Quite busy.' He hefted bags of cement into the back of the van. 'Was that Mr Towers I saw go into the house?'

'Yes,' she nodded. Why had she never noticed the respect everyone had when talking about or to Jerome? The people around here were a close-knit bunch, and for him to have made such an impression meant that she had been totally wrong about him. She had been letting her prejudices blind her. But not any more! Now her eyes were wide open—and the pain of loving him was even worse than disliking him. 'He's come to see your father,' she explained.

Donald didn't seem surprised by this information. 'Dad should be back at work soon. Another few weeks, the doctor said.'

'I suppose you'll be relieved,' she said lightly. 'It can't have been very easy on you and Patsy this last few months.'

He shrugged. 'I'm okay, and Patsy has Mum for company when I'm not around.'

'Your mother? But surely——'

'Didn't you know, Patsy and I have been living here since Dad had his attack.'

'Here?' she echoed sharply. 'You're living here?'

'Mm. It isn't the ideal situation, we have to sleep in

the lounge every night, but we should be able to move back to our own home soon. I thought it better to stay here, my mother needed me.'

And what about Patsy? Poor Patsy, no wonder she had turned to another man! She and Donald could only have been married a few weeks when Tam had his heart attack, and knowing how small and cramped these cottages could be she could sympathise with them. It certainly wasn't the ideal situation, as Donald had said it wasn't—far from it, she would have said. They would have absolutely no privacy, and Donald's little brother—who obviously occupied the second bedroom—was a mischievous little wretch. He probably took great delight in taunting the newly married couple, and in Patsy's already nervous state that could be disastrous to the relationship.

She almost groaned as she saw Patsy come out of the cottage, a furiously resentful look in her eyes. 'Why didn't you come into the house, Megan?' her voice was brittle. 'You could have had a cup of coffee while you waited for Mr Towers.'

Megan smiled. 'That would have been nice, but Mr Towers said he wasn't going to be long.'

'He's a busy man.' Donald loaded the last of the cement. 'It's good of him to call at all.' He bent to kiss Patsy briefly on the mouth. 'See you later, love. 'Bye, Megan.'

'What have you been saying to him?' Patsy turned furiously on her once Donald had driven off.

Megan frowned. 'Saying to him . . .? Oh, I see,' she nodded understanding. 'I haven't said anything to him at all. It isn't my business to tell him.'

'I would have thought you would have enjoyed it. It would have given you your revenge.'

'Revenge?' Megan shook her head in puzzlement.

'Why on earth should I want revenge on you?'

'Because of Roddy, because he prefers me to you.'

Megan gave a choked laugh. 'I don't want him!'

'Liar!' Patsy said vehemently. 'He told me all about you, about how you were after all the men on your ward at the hospital, about how annoyed you were because he wasn't interested.'

'Wasn't——? Patsy——'

'He still isn't interested,' her eyes flashed deeply blue. 'So just keep your hands off him!'

'Patsy——'

'But of course, you have your eye on Mr Towers now, don't you? Can't you find a man of your own?'

Megan flinched from the hatred in the other girl's face. 'Can't you stick with the one you've got?' she retorted insultingly, realising that reasoning wasn't going to get her anywhere with the incensed Patsy.

'Donald?' Patsy flushed. 'I—He doesn't understand.'

'I'm not surprised! I doubt if any man would understand adultery by his wife.'

'I haven't committed adultery!' Patsy was outraged. 'Roddy and I are—friends.'

'That isn't a new name for it,' Megan scorned.

'We're friends!' Patsy told her fiercely. 'Ask Roddy, he——'

'He seems to think you're going to be a lot more than that any day now,' Megan took a chance on Patsy's basic insecurity, watching the other girl's quick frown, the flash of uncertainty in her eyes. 'He boasted of it to me only yesterday,' she played on Patsy's momentary weakness. 'He means to get you into bed with him, Patsy,' she added gently.

'No!' Patsy bit her lip. 'I—I don't believe you. He—I—We're just friends. *Friends!*'

'I don't buy that, Patsy, and neither will Donald if he

finds out you've been meeting Roddy.'

Patsy's eyes narrowed. 'Are you going to tell him?' she asked with suspicion.

Megan shook her head. 'I'm no blackmailer. Patsy, what possessed you to become involved with him? Donald's a nice boy, very hardworking, and he loves you very much.'

'I know,' Patsy said heavily. 'And I love him. But— It's been so awkward, living here,' she explained in a rush. 'Tam had his heart attack only three weeks after the wedding, and Donald decided we should move in here to help his mum all we could. At the time I agreed that it was the only thing to do. But now—well ... Tam gets restless in the night, you see, and he wanders around the cottage.' Her face was fiery red. 'It's got to the stage where I daren't let Donald touch me, just in case his father walks in.'

'And that's why you've turned to Roddy?' It would be just like him to take advantage of such a situation!

'I haven't—Yes,' Patsy sighed. 'He—he flatters me, makes me feel good.'

'But is he worth losing Donald?' Megan probed gently.

'No!' there was genuine horror in Patsy's eyes. 'You're right,' she said heavily. 'I've been behaving stupidly. But it's never gone further than a few kisses between Roddy and myself. You do believe that?'

'I believe it,' Megan nodded.

'And you won't tell Donald?'

'I've already said I won't. But if you're sensible you'll stop seeing Roddy. And I'm not telling you that because I'm jealous,' she put in hurriedly. 'I'm really not interested in Roddy.'

Patsy frowned. 'But he said——'

'I can imagine what he said,' Megan interrupted

dryly. 'Roddy likes to think he can have any girl he wants. When I made it obvious I wasn't interested he turned nasty.'

'But he said——'

'Yes?' Megan queried sharply as Patsy broke off in mid-sentence.

'He said you were dismissed from the hospital,' she revealed reluctantly. 'That you were found in your room in bed with one of your patients.'

Megan gasped, her face pale. 'He told you that?'

'Is it true?' Patsy sounded incredulous.

'No!' Megan told her vehemently. 'Well—partly true, I suppose. But the man wasn't an invited guest, he tried to force himself on me. Unfortunately no one believed my side of the story.'

'So you got the sack.'

'Asked to leave,' Megan confirmed. She turned as she heard Jerome making his farewells to the senior Jones. 'Now you will finish with Roddy? Promise me.'

'I—Yes, I will.'

'Tonight,' she pressured as she heard Jerome's footsteps on the gravel behind her.

'Yes,' Patsy nodded her head vigorously, also conscious of his approach.

Megan looked up and gave Jerome a dazzling smile. 'Are we leaving now?'

He studied her with narrowed eyes. 'If you're ready . . .?'

Megan felt quite pleased with herself on the way back to The Towers; at least she had persuaded Patsy to stop seeing Roddy.

'You were talking to Patsy for some time,' Jerome remarked casually.

Her blush was almost one of guilt. 'We were at school together,' she said defensively.

'Nice girl.'

'Yes,' she agreed warily.

'Happily married.'

'Yes.' Megan frowned, wondering where all this was leading to. He hadn't realised that Patsy was Roddy's secret date, had he? Oh, she hoped not, not now that it was to end.

Jerome quirked one eyebrow. 'And wanting to remain so, I presume?'

'Yes.' Had her reply been made too vigorously? It would seem so, by the hard look he gave her.

'Warning you off, was she?'

'Warning——? What do you mean?' Oh heavens, he had realised!

He gave her a look of disgust. 'I never thought when you eliminated Roddy and Paul from your life that there was yet another contender—and I don't mean me.'

Megan gasped. 'Then who——?'

'Donald Jones!' he said grimly.

'Donald . . .?'

'Yes, Donald! Is he the reason Roddy was so angry this morning?' he demanded to know.

'You have it all wrong, Jerome,' she shook her head dazedly.

'No, I think I finally have it all right,' he corrected harshly, reaching past her to push open her door as they reached The Towers. 'Get out of my sight!' His mouth twisted. 'You leave a bad taste in my mouth.'

'Jerome . . .' She got out of the Range Rover just before he put his foot down hard on the accelerator, her car door slamming with the force of it. She watched miserably as the vehicle screeched out of the driveway and away from the house.

Stella Mitchell came out of the lounge as Megan

entered the house. 'Oh, I thought I heard Rome,' she tried to hide her disappointment behind her friendly smile. 'Do you have any idea where he is?' she asked brightly.

Megan was still dazed by Jerome's wrong assumption. 'I—I think he still had some checking up to do. He brought me back because I—I should be helping Mrs Reece this afternoon.'

'Oh yes,' Stella nodded, 'Rome told me of the deal he'd made with you——'

'With my brother,' Megan corrected fiercely. 'I had little to do with it.'

'Oh,' the other woman frowned. 'Maybe I got it wrong, then. I have a terrible head for business.'

'So do I. If you'll excuse me, Miss Mitchell . . .' Megan said pointedly, anxious to escape.

'But of course,' Stella smiled again. 'I'm sorry I delayed you.'

Megan hurried away. Every time the other woman called Jerome 'Rome' she emphasised the difference in their relationships towards him. Stella Mitchell was allowed the intimacy of his family name, whereas she was still calling him 'Mr Towers'. Oh, how that hurt her!

She stopped with her hand outstretched to push open the kitchen door, arrested in the action by the conversation she could hear behind the door.

'But Roddy said that Megan——'

'Mr Roddy to you,' Freda sternly cut in on the young maid's chatter. 'And I don't want to hear what he says. Megan is a fine girl. I don't care what Mr Roddy told you, he must have got it wrong.'

'Then why did she leave the hospital so quickly?' Connie asked.

'Maybe she just didn't like it,' Freda dismissed abruptly. 'I'm sure she wasn't dismissed—and especially for the reason you've just said.'

'But——'

'Stop your chattering, Connie, and get on with your work. And I want no more gossip about Megan in my hearing. She's a good girl, and Mr Roddy is mistaken about that man being in her bedroom.'

Megan was deathly pale. Roddy had said he would make her pay, and it seemed his vengeance had already started. She wondered how long it would take Jerome to hear this latest little slur on her character. Not long, if Roddy had anything to do with it.

CHAPTER SEVEN

MEGAN was feeling very nervous the next morning as she waited for Jerome to put in an appearance. Once again he was late, and Freda had told her that this was because he had arrived late back from his work on the estate and so was breakfasting late. There was nothing for Megan to do, Jerome wouldn't let her open the mail herself, so she sat on the sofa in front of the glowing fire, feeling more like a schoolgirl awaiting punishment in the headmaster's office than a secretary simply waiting for her boss.

Yesterday had been a disaster from start to finish, not least being the fact that she had had to tell Paul she wouldn't marry him. He had come round in the evening and they had gone out for a drink together. As soon as he began discussing marriage she knew she would have to put a stop to it. He had been hurt and angry, and Megan had felt awful. But better to let him down now than later.

'Dreaming, Miss Finch?' taunted a familiar voice.

Megan looked up from the fire and rose agilely to her feet. 'I didn't know what to do,' she said lamely.

Jerome was dressed more formally than usual, the charcoal-grey suit and matching tie complemented by the snowy white shirt. He looked formidable and unapproachable, and Megan picked up her notepad with shaking fingers.

'Didn't Freda tell you I'd been delayed?' He moved around the desk and sat down to begin opening the mail.

'Yes. But I—You told me not to touch your mail.' He had told her that her first day here, much to Megan's annoyance. It made it seem as if he didn't trust her.

He pinpointed her with his dark brown eyes. 'I shall be going to London this morning for several days, so you'll have to deal with some of the mail. Anything you can't handle put to one side and I'll see to it when I get back.'

Megan's eyes were wide. 'You're going away?'

'Back to London with Miss Mitchell,' he confirmed haughtily. 'I'll leave my telephone number in case you need to get in touch with me.'

But would Stella Mitchell be the one to answer such a call? Did Jerome live with the other woman while he was in London? It certainly looked like it. 'Very well,' Megan acknowledged tautly.

'How are the arrangements for the Christmas party going?' he asked.

For a moment Megan looked blank. The children's Christmas party was the last thing on her mind. 'I—er—I called the nursery about the tree, and arranged for the caterers to provide the necessary furniture. It seems Freda likes to do the food herself.'

Jerome frowned. 'Isn't it a bit much for her?'

Megan shrugged. 'That's what I said, but she insisted. And Mrs Reece told me Freda loves doing it, that she looks forward to it each year.'

'Oh well,' he shrugged. 'If that's what she wants.'

'I—er—I found your costume for you,' a teasing light entered her eyes. 'It was in the wardrobe of one of the spare bedrooms.'

'I just can't see myself as Father Christmas,' he grimaced. 'Can't we get someone else to do it?'

'Of course not!' She sounded scandalised. 'It's traditional for the owner of The Towers to do it. The costume will need some padding out on you,' she indicated his taut, flat stomach. 'Old Squire Towers never needed any,' she remembered with a smile.

'You liked him, didn't you?' Jerome said softly.

'He could be cantankerous.' Megan hadn't realised quite how much until Jerome had told her the reason for his dislike of him. 'But yes, I think I did like him. I used to visit him here. Of course it was all different then, threadbare carpets and worn furniture.'

Jerome scowled. 'The old man let Ralph Coates rob him blind,' he muttered angrily.

'Ralph Coates? You mean the last estate manager?'

He nodded. 'My uncle left too much to the other man, trusted him too much. He repaid him by fiddling the books.'

'And that's why you sacked him?'

Mocking humour lightened Jerome's expression. 'Another of your grudges against me dashed to the ground?' he taunted.

Megan flushed. 'I didn't realise Ralph was a thief.'

'I'm sure you found it easier to imagine I'd dismissed him without reason. Don't be upset, Megan,' he drawled as she went to protest. 'Honest dislike is a healthy thing.'

She looked down at her hands. 'Not if it's given unfairly.'

'Are you saying I could be wrong about you?' his eyes were narrowed.

Megan's gaze was challenging. 'Couldn't you?'

His mouth twisted. 'No,' he said emphatically. 'I've kissed you myself, Megan. I know the way you react, and it isn't the reaction of a shy young virgin.'

She was well aware that she had acted like a wanton in his arms, but she had never acted that way with anyone else. 'I didn't say I was shy,' she said pointedly.

'You aren't a virgin either!' Jerome scorned. 'Shall we deal with this mail,' he added briskly. 'I have to leave soon.'

Megan glared at him. 'You've just sat there and insulted me and now you calmly propose to dictate your mail to me?' She stood angrily to her feet. 'Well, you can go to hell, Mr Towers! Our deal is null and void. I won't work for you any longer!'

He moved swiftly, slamming the door shut as she opened it. He pinned her against the back of the door, towering darkly over her. 'You really are a selfish little——'

'That's right,' she choked, closing her eyes to hide her tears, biting her bottom lip to stop it trembling, 'insult me some more! I have no way of defending myself, I just have to stand here and take that from you.'

'You can take this too!' He lowered his head with a groan, his lips surprisingly gentle as they parted hers.

His body lowered against her, his hardened thighs, intimate against hers, telling her better than any words how aroused he was. Megan wanted to take his kisses, wanted his arms about her, wanted to be roused to the passion that only he could kindle in her.

They were lost in a world of lovemaking, each kiss

more drugging than the last, Megan's groans of pleasure inciting Jerome to even more intimacies.

'Your breasts,' he moaned against her silky skin, her blouse unbuttoned to his questing fingers. 'They're the most beautiful thing I've ever seen. God, I even dreamt about you last night.' His tongue caressed one taut nipple. 'The things I imagined doing to you! Do you give the same pleasure to all your men?' he wanted to know. 'Do they get turned on just watching you walk, watching the way you move, the way the material of your blouse stretches across your wonderful breasts?'

'Jerome, please! Don't say things like that,' she begged, making ineffectual movements to push him away, blushing as she thought of him watching her so intimately. He gave no indication of these thoughts normally, and it was now embarrassing to know what he had been thinking all this time. 'I don't deliberately draw attention to myself,' she denied.

'You don't need to,' he said huskily. 'I know the exact moment you walk into a room, can gauge your mood immediately. Right now you want to make love as badly as I do.'

'No . . .'

'Yes, Megan.' He kissed her lightly on the lips, doing the buttons back up on her blouse. 'Why do we always choose the study for making love?' he queried wryly. 'I prefer the comfort of a bed, and the added knowledge that no one is going to walk in on us.'

'I'm sure you've had plenty of practice,' she said sharply.

'Rule number one, Megan,' he tapped her playfully on the nose, 'I won't delve into your past if you won't delve into mine. Agreed?'

'Miss Mitchell isn't exactly your past!'

'She will be this time tomorrow. Rule number two,'

he said seriously, 'I don't like to share. Stella goes out of my life and so Donald, Paul, Roddy, and any other men I don't know about go out of yours.'

'They aren't in my life!' She frowned. 'Jerome, what are all these rules leading to?'

He eyed her mockingly, straightening his tie. 'Never been propositioned quite so bluntly before?' he taunted. 'I don't think you'll find me ungenerous, and I'm not usually very demanding of your time—just a few hours a week, although in your case it might be different. Think you can stand the pace?'

'The pace?' she repeated numbly. 'I don't know what you're talking about.'

'I want you, Megan Finch, and I mean to have you.'

She gaped at him. 'But yesterday you told me—you said I leave a bad taste in your mouth!'

'Mm,' he scowled darkly. 'Well, you haven't been very discriminating. Did no one ever tell you not to get involved with married men? In a village this size Patsy was sure to find out about you and Donald.'

'Mr Towers——'

'Rome,' he corrected huskily. 'When I get back from London we're going to become very close. I think you'll find my sex-drive is more than twice a week,' he added tauntingly.

Megan blushed fiery red. 'Are you suggesting—are you asking me to be your mistress?'

'This is the time of equality; mistress sounds too subservient.' His gaze was warm on her. 'And subservience is the last thing I want from you.'

'When did you—when did you decide to have an affair with me?' She was dazed by his audacity.

'When I realised that it was jealousy that was making me so angry with you,' he admitted ruefully.

'Jealousy . . .?'

'Yes,' he smiled. 'Pretty basic stuff, but enough to tell me I want you in my bed.'

Jealousy should have implied love, but to this man it only showed a need to possess for himself. 'And how will we conduct this affair? Book into some seedy hotel for the night when you get the urge to take me?' Megan's tone was bitter.

'Where do you usually go to bed with your men? Oh, of course, you had a room at the hospital,' he answered his own question. 'Very convenient for you.'

'Very,' she replied through stiff lips. 'Except that men weren't allowed into the nurses' home.'

'I doubt that ever stopped them. Look, I have to go now, we'll sort out the details when I get back. But we aren't going to meet in a hotel,' he added firmly. 'Seedy or otherwise.'

'I don't——' Someone was trying to open the door! Megan panicked, looking to Jerome for help. 'What shall we do?' she asked desperately.

'Let them in, of course,' he said calmly. 'It's probably Stella. I said we would leave about ten, and it's that now.'

'But I—lord, I must look a mess!' She made an effort to tidy her hair.

'Stop panicking,' Jerome ceased her movements. 'You look beautiful, very kissed and desirable.'

'That's the last thing I want to look! I don't want Miss Mitchell to know that we——'

'She already knows, Megan. Don't look like that,' he soothed. 'She isn't likely to scratch your eyes out. I had to give her some excuse for not sharing her bed this visit. Unlike you, I find it difficult to sleep with one person while desiring another. In fact, I find it impossible.'

'Unlike me——?' she echoed.

'You and I have wanted each other since the first day we met, and yet you've still been seeing other men. That can all stop when I get back, I like to know I have exclusive rights during the time of my interest.'

'You——'

'Rome?' Stella Mitchell's voice queried, and the door-handle rattled again. 'Rome, are you in there?'

He put Megan firmly to one side and opened the door. 'Come in, Stella. Megan and I were just discussing my return. Are you ready to leave?' he looked at the red-haired woman enquiringly.

Stella looked from one to the other of them, obviously noting Megan's flushed face and Jerome's warm gaze on that bent blonde head. 'Yes, I'm ready,' she said brightly.

'I just have to see Jeff before we leave. Wait for me here,' he instructed.

'Oh, but——' Megan's plea for help went unheeded. She looked almost guiltily at Stella Mitchell, although what she had to feel guilty about she didn't know. Jerome Towers should be the one to feel guilty for suggesting such an idea to her. 'I—I didn't realise you were going back to London today,' she said awkwardly to the other woman, wondering exactly what Jerome had told her.

Stella looked as coolly beautiful as usual, the green of her woollen suit exactly matching her eyes. 'It was all rather sudden,' she acknowledged. 'I'm sure you know why.'

'I—Why, no, I——'

'It's all right, Megan,' Stella smiled. 'I've always known I was a replaceable commodity in Rome's life. I've done well to last this long.'

Megan frowned. 'But don't you *mind*? I would hate it,' she shuddered.

'We made no ties on each other. When I met Rome I was just getting over a very nasty divorce, and his undemanding relationship, emotionally, was just what I needed. Now I think maybe I'm ready to fall in love again.'

'But not with Rome?'

She shook her head. 'He wouldn't thank me for it. It's something he doesn't have time for. I believe I lasted this long because he knew there was no danger of my falling in love with him. Most of his women do, you know, and then they're instantly out of his life.' Her expression softened sympathetically. 'Don't let him know you love him, Megan. Love is a tie he won't accept.'

Megan was very pale. 'You *know* I love him?'

'Oh yes. I don't think he's realised yet, so make the most of him before he does find out. He's a considerate lover, Megan, completely unselfish. My husband was the opposite, that's why being with Rome has been so wonderful.'

'Are you sure you don't love him?' Megan probed. 'You sound as if you do.'

Stella flushed. 'Well . . . maybe a little. I'll always love him, but I'm not *in* love with him. I could have been, I'm not denying that, but Rome never gave any indication of feeling that way about me, and when love isn't returned it soon dies. Love has to be nurtured, encouraged, and I never got any of that from Rome. He's cut me out of the intimate side of his life now, but we'll remain friends. Will you mind that? I can assure you he'll never sleep with me again.'

'I'm not going to have an affair with him, Miss Mitchell,' Megan said tautly. '*Miss* Mitchell?' she queried in a puzzled voice.

Stella shrugged. 'My maiden name. When my husband and I divorced I didn't want anything that reminded me of him, including his name.'

'I see. Well, I'm not going to have an affair with Rome, no matter what he may think to the contrary.'

Stella gave her a probing look. 'When Rome has that look of determination in his eyes there's no one who can stop him getting what he wants, and he wants you.'

'He isn't getting me!' Megan said fiercely.

Stella laughed, a laugh of complete enjoyment. 'I wish I could stay around and watch the battle of wills. It looks as if it could prove quite entertaining.'

'There won't be a battle,' she denied. 'I shall just tell him no.'

'And you think he'll just accept that?' Stella shook her head pityingly. 'Rome's never heard of the word no.'

'He'll hear it from me!'

Stella eyed her teasingly. 'Did you say no to him just now?'

Megan flushed. 'Well . . . I——'

'Lethal, isn't he?' Stella laughed. 'I like you, Megan. Make Rome happy,' she added softly. 'He deserves to be, he's the kindest man I've ever known.'

'I've never found him in the least kind!'

'He will be. At the moment he finds it difficult to even be in the same room with you. I knew what was happening the first time I saw the two of you together, sparks seem to fly every time you meet.'

'Yes,' Megan admitted huskily.

'You're going to lose, Megan,' the other woman told her gently. 'Better to give in gracefully.'

'Never!'

Jerome appeared in the open doorway, his eyes narrowed as he looked at them both. 'All right?' he asked generally.

At that moment Megan realised that Jerome had deliberately left her alone with Stella, had wanted to prove to her that the other woman bore no grudge. Would she be subjected to the same humiliation when he decided to replace her in a few months' time? She could never be so complacent about losing Jerome as Stella was being, would indeed want to 'scratch the eyes out' of any replacement he had for her.

Stella gave him a warm smile. 'Yes, fine. I'll wait outside in the car, shall I?'

'Thanks, Stella.' Jerome was watching Megan closely. 'Having second thoughts?' he asked softly once they were alone.

'I didn't think I'd had first ones,' she said resentfully.

'I had enough for both of us,' he smiled. 'Most of them erotic.'

'Rome, I—Jerome,' she corrected firmly. 'You can't be serious about this?'

'Don't be absurd,' he said tersely. 'You know damn well I'm serious. We're both adults, Megan, and I'm too old to play childish games. I want you, you want me, so we take the logical course to satisfy both of us.' His eyes narrowed. 'You don't like the fact that I object to your other men, is that it? I won't share, Megan, it isn't in my nature.'

'It isn't that,' she said indignantly. 'Do you realise that Stella is perfectly happy to just fade out of your life?'

'We made no promises to each other,' he accepted arrogantly.

'And I suppose you would expect me to accept my dismissal as quietly as that?' Her eyes flashed with temper. 'When you're tired of me, of course.'

Jerome gave a husky laugh. 'I wouldn't expect you to

accept anything. It's your fiery nature that attracted me in the first place. We'll deal with the severing of our relationship when the time comes, if it comes.' He kissed her softly on the lips, reluctantly moving away from her. 'I'll call you from London. Maybe you could even join me at the weekend?'

'But won't you be back by then?'

'I doubt it.' He picked up his briefcase, now the epitome of the English businessman. 'There's been a strike called at one of my factories. It's better if I deal with the situation myself, and these disputes have been known to last weeks. Will you come up to London if I make the arrangements?'

'To start our affair?' she queried bitterly.

He shrugged, obviously impatient to leave. 'Is there any point in our waiting?'

'Yes, there's a point! I have no intention——'

'I have to go now, Megan,' he gave a hurried glance at the plain gold watch on his wrist. 'I'll call you.' This time his kiss was hard before he quickly left the house.

Megan's protest about there not going to be an affair had been ignored by Jerome. She was left with the feeling of having been swept off her feet, of being cornered into a relationship she had no intention of entering. She didn't have affairs, had never had an affair, and the fact that she loved Jerome did not make this an exception.

As she walked into the yard of their farm later that evening she saw their tractor had been returned and the nice shiny new model they had borrowed from The Towers had been taken back.

'No Brian?' she asked her mother as she sat down for her meal.

'Been and gone.' Her mother joined her at the table, only a cup of tea in front of her. 'I ate with him, I hope you don't mind.'

'No, I don't mind. Where's he gone?'

'Back to work.' Her mother shrugged. 'There's still a few hours daylight left yet.'

'Did Paul go with him?' she asked casually.

'Yes. He's a good boy, is Paul. You told him, didn't you?' her mother probed gently.

Megan sighed. 'I had to, Mum. He started talking about weddings, where we would live afterwards. He had even asked Jeff Robbins if there would be a cottage vacant on the estate for us.'

'And was there?'

'No, thank goodness!' I let him down gently, as you said I should, but he still seemed to take it hard.' In fact he had slammed out of the house shortly after nine o'clock, and she hadn't heard from him since.

'He'll get over it. It's you I'm worried about,' her mother frowned her concern.

'Me?' Megan looked genuinely surprised. 'Why on earth are you worried about me?'

'I don't like you working at The Towers.'

'But I thought we'd all agreed that it wouldn't matter for six months?'

'It isn't the work I object to.' Her mother looked uncomfortable, her expression prim. 'I don't like the way he looks at you,' she said in a rush. 'It isn't decent.'

Megan flushed and bit her lip. 'And how does he look at me?' So even though she hadn't noticed Jerome's interest, her mother had!

'You know . . .' her mother said coyly.

'No,' Megan denied with feigned innocence.

'He—well, he—It just isn't right, Megan.' Her mother was becoming flustered now. 'If Mr Towers should see him——'

'Mr Towers?' Megan echoed sharply. 'Who are we

talking about? I thought you meant——'

'Certainly not Mr Towers!' her mother was scandalised at the suggestion. 'He's a gentleman, not like that brother of his.'

'Oh, Roddy.' Megan sighed understanding. 'Yes, he's far from being a gentleman.' And so was Jerome when it came to getting a woman he desired!

'The way he looks at you,' her mother shuddered. 'It's disgusting!'

'I'm not interested in him, Mum, so you have nothing to fear.'

'With his sort they don't need any encouragement!'

Megan laughed as naturally as she could, glad that someone else could sense the danger in Roddy. 'Go and get ready for your meeting this evening. The treasurer of the Women's Institute shouldn't be late,' she teased.

'You just watch out for that Roddy Meyers,' her mother advised, standing up. 'I don't trust him.'

Neither did Megan. She hadn't seen him all day and had wondered, had hoped, that perhaps he had gone back to London too. When he rang for his tea at four-thirty she realised he hadn't, and although she got Connie to take the tray through, unwilling to see him herself, Connie had come back with a high colour on her cheeks, and Megan had drawn her own conclusions.

'How's it going?' she asked Brian later that evening, relieved that he had returned alone. Another scene with Paul was the last thing she needed at the moment.

He shrugged. 'Bit soon to tell. Although we're certainly getting the work done with the two of us at it.'

'I see we have our tractor back.'

Brian grimaced. 'For what it's worth.'

'Did it cost much to repair?'

'Not too bad,' he shrugged.

Megan looked at him closely. 'But we had enough money to pay for it?'

'Here's the bill,' he handed it to her. 'You can see it has "paid" stamped across it. I'm just going up to wash and change before going over to see Joyce.'

'But, Brian——' Too late, he had already disappeared up the stairs.

Megan frowned over the amount the repair work had cost. She was sure they didn't have this sort of money. So if they hadn't paid it, who had? The answer wasn't a pleasant one.

'Brian,' she stopped him as he would have dashed out of the house, 'did Mr Towers pay this bill?' She still held it in her hand.

'How could he?' he evaded. 'He's in London today.'

'Yes, but we don't have as much money as this, I know that. If Mr Towers didn't pay for it himself then he arranged to have it paid. Am I right?' she persisted.

Her brother sighed. 'Completely,' he admitted.

'Oh, Brian!' she groaned. 'I don't like being in debt to him.' It put her under too much of an obligation to him herself, and in the circumstances that wasn't a good thing!

'I didn't have any other way of paying it, Megan.' His voice was almost pleading. 'Mr Towers offered and . . . I'm going to pay him back as soon as I get the money together.'

'And when will that be?'

'I have no idea,' he answered truthfully. 'But he doesn't mind waiting for it.'

'I'm sure he doesn't. We owe him too much already, Brian. It isn't good to owe so much to one man.'

'He isn't going to suddenly demand his money back, Megan,' Brian scorned. 'He won't even miss those few paltry pounds. I must go now, I'll see you later.'

Megan stared moodily into the fire once her brother had gone. Jerome might not ask for his money back, but he could ask for his pound of flesh—*her* flesh! She couldn't possibly refuse him when they owed him so much. There was a loud hammering on the door later that evening, and Megan rose half asleep from her chair to answer it.

Roddy Meyers pushed his way past her into the house. 'Are you alone?' he growled.

She didn't like his mood, and wished she could say someone was with her. 'I—er——'

'Are you?' His fingers bit painfully into her arm.

'Yes!' She winced from the pain he was causing.

'Good, then we can talk without interruption.' He strode into the lounge.

Megan followed him, switching on the main light and so alleviating the shadowed intimacy of the room. 'What do you mean by bursting in here like this?' she demanded to know. 'I don't want you here. I want you to leave,' and she held the door open as if to prove her point.

Roddy ignored her, his eyes narrowed with anger. 'You couldn't leave it alone, could you?' he scowled. 'You had to interfere!'

Megan frowned her puzzlement. 'I don't know what you're talking about.'

'I mean Patsy,' he snapped. 'She's just told me that she doesn't want to see me any more, that she and her husband are moving back to their own home.'

'Good for Patsy!' Megan smiled her pleasure.

'Why did you interfere?' Roddy demanded. 'Was it because you were jealous?'

'Jealous? Of what?'

'Of her. Would you rather it was you who went out with me?'

She gave an incredulous laugh. 'Certainly not!'

Roddy went white with rage. 'Then why did you break Patsy and me up?'

'For her sake, not yours.'

'Then you can damn well pay for your interference!' he told her furiously.

She could tell he meant it, knew that it wasn't just an idle threat. Roddy didn't make idle threats, he was a very dangerous man. 'How?' she asked warily.

'Use your imagination, Megan,' he taunted. 'Things were progressing very nicely with Patsy. You put an end to that, so now you can take her place.'

'I can——?' she gasped. 'Roddy, I think you're slightly mad! I have no intention of seeing you any more than I have to.'

'Now that's a shame, because I have every intention of seeing you.'

'Not if I don't want you to,' she snapped.

'How about if I threaten to tell Donald Jones of the affair I've had with his wife?' Roddy asked calmly.

Megan gasped. 'You wouldn't!'

His stance was challenging. 'Try me.'

CHAPTER EIGHT

HER second caller that night wasn't so much angry as upset. Patsy had tears streaming down her cheeks, her distress was obvious.

'Oh, Megan!' she collapsed into her arms, stumbling into the house. 'Oh God, I don't know what I'm going to do,' she sobbed.

Megan guided her over to a chair and seated herself

on the arm. 'The first thing you're going to do is calm down,' she soothed. 'Come on, Patsy, whatever it is it can't be as bad as you think it is.' Although she very much had the feeling that it was worse, much worse.

'It's Roddy,' Patsy confirmed her fears. 'I thought about what you said, and then I—I told him that I thought it better if we didn't meet any more. He was furious, but then I expected that. Then he became very calm, very understanding all of a sudden. I was just so relieved I didn't question his reaction. Then a little while ago he telephoned me,' she began to tremble. 'He was vile, Megan!' she shuddered. 'I don't know how I could ever have been attracted to him.'

'Go on,' Megan encouraged.

'Well, at first I was stunned. He called me right there at Donald's parents' house. Tam answered the phone,' she revealed shakily. 'I told him it was my brother, although I'm not sure he believed me.'

'What did Roddy have to say?' Megan prompted.

Patsy frowned. 'Lots of things, but the main thing was that he intends telling Donald about us.'

Megan chewed on her bottom lip. 'Do you think Donald will believe him?'

The other girl flushed. 'Yes.'

Megan gave her a sharp look. 'How can you be so sure?'

'Donald and I—we haven't been getting on too well lately. I—well, I told you what it was like there! I just can't respond to Donald in that house.' She blushed. 'Donald's been teasing me the last few weeks, saying that maybe I have another man and that's why I'm not interested in him.'

'I see,' Megan sighed. This was getting worse, not better. 'But you did say it was only teasing, I'm sure Donald didn't mean it.'

'Of course he didn't. But he's been worried about me. He even made me stop work at The Towers because he said it was too much for me. I was furious at the time, but I'm glad of it now. If I'd stayed on there I would probably have—well, I would have more to regret now than I actually do,' Patsy admitted blushingly.

'Why did you come to see me, Patsy?'

'Because you're the only person I can turn to, the only person I can talk to. If Roddy tells Donald it won't matter that nothing—physical happened between us. Donald will look at the facts, and after he's beaten Roddy up he'll throw me out. I may have been stupid, Megan, but I don't want to lose Donald.'

'You aren't going to lose him,' Megan told her firmly. 'I'll talk to Roddy for you.'

'Oh, would you?' Patsy's expression brightened.

'Yes. I'm sure I can make him see reason. He's probably just feeling bitter at your change of mind,' Megan excused, knowing that he was nothing of the sort, still trembling from her own encounter with him. 'He'll come round,' she soothed.

'Do you really think so?' Patsy was eager to be re-assured now.

'Yes, I do. Now you tidy yourself up and get back home. There's no point in arousing Donald's suspicions at this late stage. Go through to the bathroom and wash your face,' Megan invited.

Damn Roddy Meyers! When she had taken up his challenge earlier she hadn't for one moment thought he would do something like this. He had her trapped, well and truly trapped.

'Better?' she asked Patsy brightly when she returned.

'Much,' the other girl smiled. 'Thanks, Megan. You've been really nice about all this.'

'Maybe you can do the same for me one day. Not

really,' Megan laughed at Patsy's expression. 'And don't worry any more about Roddy. I'll deal with him.'

'Donald and I are going back to our own cottage tomorrow. Tam's a lot better, so Donald has agreed to leave.'

Megan squeezed her hand. 'I hope it all works out for you. And, Patsy,' she halted her exit, 'no more Roddy Meyers, hmm?'

'Never!' Patsy vowed. 'I'll only be that kind of fool once.' She looked a little happier as she left.

Megan was beginning to realise that *she* had been all kinds of a fool where Roddy was concerned. She had underestimated him, hadn't realised just how cunning and cruel he could be.

When the telephone began ringing shortly before ten o'clock she knew it had to be him, calling to gloat. 'Yes?' she snapped into the receiver.

'Who's upset you?' drawled a caressingly familiar voice.

'Rome!' she cried her relief.

'Megan . . .' he groaned. 'God, why can't you say my name like that when we're together, and not wait until we're miles apart and I can't touch you!'

She had been so relieved to hear his voice, her emotions were unguarded as her love for him clamoured for release. 'How are things going?' she asked huskily, longing for his return.

'Deadlock,' he sighed. 'A bit like our own relationship, really.'

She blushed, although of course he couldn't see that. 'The negotiations aren't going well?' She ignored his personal reference.

Rome gave a husky laugh, well aware of her omission. 'They aren't going at all. They tell me what they want, I tell them what they can have, then we both retreat to our corners and come out fighting.'

'So it looks like being a long struggle?' she asked with dismay.

'Dare I hope that you're missing me?'

More than he would ever know! 'I could be,' she evaded.

'I see you've retreated to your corner too,' he derided. 'I've only just got back from a meeting that's been going on all day, a meeting that turned out to be a complete waste of time, so I would be grateful if I didn't get the same cold front from you.'

'What do these men want?'

'What they usually want,' he sighed. 'Money.'

'Can't you give it to them?' He seemed rich enough.

'If I give in this time they'll expect me to give in every time they decide they want a raise. I've offered them ten per cent, they've asked for twenty, we both know we'll settle somewhere in between.'

He sounded very tired, and Megan's heart went out to him. 'Well, if you both know that why don't you settle now?'

'It's easy to tell you've never been in business! It just isn't done that way.'

'But why isn't it?'

'Don't ask me,' he sighed. 'Ask them. All I can say is that it's happened at a very inconvenient time for me. I can't begin to concentrate on these negotiations when I have you so much on my mind. Have you thought any more about this weekend?'

She hadn't had the time! Not that she really needed it, she already knew her answer. 'I've thought about it,' she told him.

'You aren't coming, are you?' Rome said heavily.

'No.'

'Then I'll come back to The Towers.'

'No!'

'What do you mean, no?' he rasped. 'Before I left——'

'I was dazzled by your lovemaking,' Megan admitted frankly. 'What woman wouldn't be? You're an expert, Jerome, and I'm as susceptible as the next woman.'

'More so than most,' he muttered.

Pain like a knife thrust shot through her. 'Exactly,' she agreed dully, knowing she had to alienate the man she loved. 'I've decided I can't be a one-man woman, not even for the short time you would want me.'

'I didn't say it would be for a short time,' he snapped.

'Well, I certainly couldn't last out a year like Stella did.' Megan was deliberately flippant. 'It just isn't my idea of fun.'

'And you like to have fun, don't you?' His voice was harsh.

'Who doesn't?' She gave a light laugh. 'Maybe you can still get Stella back if you hurry.'

There was a long angry silence. 'I don't want Stella!' he finally exploded.

'Didn't your mother ever tell you that you can't have everything you want?' she taunted.

'She may have mentioned it.'

'Then you should know it isn't good for you to have your own way all the time. Now if you'll excuse me, I think I hear someone at the door,' she invented.

'This time of night?'

'It's still early yet.'

'And will it be Donald, Roddy, or Paul?' Jerome rasped.

'Oh, definitely Roddy.'

'Roddy! But you said——'

'It's a woman's prerogative to change her mind,' she cut in. 'Roddy can be quite—entertaining.'

She wasn't surprised to hear the receiver slam down at the other end. She slumped down into a chair, sobs racking her body. Jerome would surely hate her now. It was what she had wanted, but it didn't make it any easier to bear.

Her face was red and blotchy by the time her tears had ceased, and even cold water didn't improve it. She decided to go for a walk, maybe the fresh air would clear her head. Besides, she had to see Roddy as soon as possible, and as she doubted he would have gone to bed yet, now seemed as good a time as any.

She was right about him not having gone to bed. He was in the lounge of The Towers listening to records, and showed no surprise when she walked into the room.

'Sit down,' he invited, almost as if he had been expecting her.

'I'd rather stand,' she refused stiffly.

'Sit down!'

With a rebellious glare in his direction she sat. 'You know why I'm here,' she snapped.

His mouth twisted. 'It doesn't take much imagination.'

Her eyes flashed her dislike as he sat facing her so calmly. 'You really are a swine,' she accused.

'Yes.'

'My God, you're proud of it!'

Roddy smiled. 'Power is a heady emotion,' he drawled. 'You should try it some time.'

'Have you forgotten the fact that I can still tell your brother about what happened at the hospital?'

He shook his head. 'I haven't forgotten at all. But in the light of your recent behaviour do you think Rome is any more likely to believe you than the hospital authorities were?'

She flushed. 'And what about your behaviour?'

'I would say we're ideally suited,' he smiled.

She shivered, hating the comparison. 'I suppose you realise you've scared Patsy half to death?'

'She deserved it,' he scowled. 'She kept me at arm's length for months.'

'She didn't keep you at arm's length, she didn't intend the relationship progressing any further than it had.'

'What do you know about it?' Roddy snapped.

'All of it,' Megan told him tightly. 'Now what do you want from me?'

'I don't want anything *from* you, I just want you.'

She flushed. 'Go to hell!'

Roddy gave a soft laugh. 'You really shouldn't make your dislike of me so obvious,' he taunted. 'You see, I like you very much. Besides, Rome wants you.'

Her eyes widened. 'And you don't want him to have me?'

'No! He has everything else,' he said viciously. 'He isn't going to get the one thing I really want.'

'Me?' she squeaked.

His eyes burnt like twin coals. 'Yes, you! Rome has all the rest, but you're mine. You see, I'm just the younger brother, the one who has to rely on Rome for every penny I spend.'

'You could always get a job.'

'Why the hell should I? Rome has millions.'

'Exactly. *Rome* has it, it isn't your money.'

'It will be when he dies.'

Megan went white. 'He's only a young man.'

Roddy shrugged. 'I can wait. If I have you the waiting won't be so bad.'

She swallowed hard. 'What if he marries, has children?'

He stood up to pour himself a drink. 'He won't.' He drank the whisky down in one gulp. 'Rome doesn't believe in marriage.'

Megan frowned. 'You don't even like him, do you?'

'Of course I like him, he's my brother! But I'm not letting him have you.' His expression was wild.

Megan was frightened. Roddy wasn't merely vindictive and cruel, he was sick. She felt sure Jerome had no idea of the finely balanced edge his brother was on, of the resentment he had stored up towards him. But she could see it, and it terrified her. If Roddy should ever hurt Jerome ... It would be her fault if he did, she could see that. Roddy was obsessed with claiming her for himself, and if Jerome tried to come in between them he would do something desperate.

But surely she must be mistaken, was seeing this situation all out of proportion. Of course Roddy wouldn't hurt his own brother.

Roddy eyed her suspiciously. 'What are you thinking now?'

'Nothing. So what happens now, do I just go out with you?'

'Isn't that enough?'

'God, yes!'

His mouth tightened. 'I'll take you out to dinner tomorrow. You never know, you could learn to like me. And stay away from my brother. He may want you, but he isn't going to get you.'

She sighed. 'He already knows that. I'll leave now. And you'll leave Patsy and Donald alone?'

'As long as you continue to go out with me.'

Megan walked slowly through the darkness, going automatically to her favourite place and sitting down on the bowed tree-trunk beside the fast-flowing river. It was very cold this time of year, and yet she needed this time here alone. What a mess!—Jerome wanting her, she wanting Jerome, and Roddy determined to make sure *he* got her. Once again that shiver of apprehension shot down her spine.

It was well after twelve as she made her way back to the farm, when the blazing headlights of the car coming towards her forced her to leap on to the grass verge for safety. There was a screech of brakes before the car started to reverse back towards her.

The passenger door to the Jaguar was thrust open. 'Get in!' Jerome ordered grimly.

She did so, looking at him dazedly. 'What are you doing here?'

He gave her a scathing look. 'Isn't it obvious?'

Megan started to thaw out a little as the warmth of the Jaguar invaded her frozen limbs. 'You should be in London,' she frowned her puzzlement.

He nodded. 'I should be at another meeting, but I had to ask my deputy to take over. I had a hell of a job getting away.'

'But why are you here?'

'Don't be stupid, Megan. You know damn well I had to see you.'

What she did know was they they were driving away from both her home and The Towers. 'Where are we going?'

'Somewhere we can talk,' he said grimly.

To Megan's surprise he drove to the spot by the river she had just left, although this time she was infinitely warmer. Jerome switched off the engine, although the heat remained. They sat for long minutes in the darkness, neither of them talking.

'What did Roddy want?' Jerome rasped suddenly.

'Roddy?' she looked puzzled. 'Oh, Roddy,' she remembered her lie of earlier. 'What do you think he wanted?' she asked suggestively.

Jerome's hands clenched around the steering-wheel,

his arms rigid as he stared straight ahead of him. 'You don't like him, I'd swear you don't.'

She shrugged. 'You said yourself, I don't have to like the man involved.'

Even in the darkness she could see the glitter of his eyes. 'You're lying, Megan. Roddy isn't trying to force you into anything, is he?'

She was glad he couldn't see how pale she had gone. 'What do you mean? I can assure you,' she regained some of her composure, 'that no man has a sexual hold over me.'

'I didn't mean that.' His gaze ran over her with fevered intensity. 'Can't you wait for me?' he asked impatiently. 'I'll only be gone a few weeks. And God knows I want you!' He pulled her into his arms, parting her lips with his own, his kiss at once arousing her.

It was as if she had been in a limbo since Jerome had left her this morning, as if she had been waiting for his touch for the inferno to ignite once again. Her arms went up about his neck, and her body arched against him as she returned the fierce pressure of his mouth.

Jerome gently nibbled her mouth, running the tip of his tongue over her sensitive inner lip. Megan quivered, longing to touch him as he had touched her in the past, straining even closer to him.

'Let's get in the back,' Jerome suggested huskily, not waiting for her answer but getting out of the car and taking her with him.

There was much more room on the back seat. Jerome pushed her down before half lying across her. How long they remained there she had no idea, but it wasn't long before she had unbuttoned his shirt, running her fingers over the hard muscle of him.

'Darling Megan,' his mouth was at her breast, her sweater no barrier to his questing hands. 'I want to love you,' he moaned into her throat. 'The perfume of you, your very essence has invaded every particle of me.' He bit her earlobe, his tongue exploring her shell-like ear and the deep hollows of her throat, shooting spasms of ecstasy through her at every caress. 'Come back to London with me?' he pleaded.

'I—I can't,' her denial was weak. 'It just isn't possible, Rome.'

'Anything is possible if you want it badly enough, and I want you more than I've ever wanted anything else in my life.' He placed light fevered kisses on every feature of her face. 'I like the feel of you, the taste of you. God, you taste so good!'

Their lips met, and an explosion of passion took them along on a tide, the darkness that surrounded them like a blanket against the rest of the world. Megan felt that they could do anything right now and it wouldn't matter. It would be a dream, their own secret happening. No one else need ever know. They could—cold reality intruded. Of all things it was the muted buzz of a telephone that interrupted them!

'A telephone?' She surfaced from Jerome's fierce embrace. 'In a car?' she asked dazedly.

He sighed. 'A necessary evil, one I intend dispensing with after tonight.' His expression was agonised; the flames of his desire still leapt in his deep brown eyes. 'It's probably Bob, my assistant. I asked him to call me if there were any new developments. Yes?' he rasped into the mouthpiece. 'Oh hell! Yes. Yes. Okay, I'll be there as quick as I can. Of course I'll damn well hurry, don't be bloody stupid!' He slammed the receiver back down again.

'What's happened?' Megan was anxious.

'They've walked out of the meeting,' he revealed grimly, hastily buttoning his shirt. 'They said they'll talk to me and no one else. They won't return to the meeting until I do. They've given me three hours to get back.'

'Oh dear. It's my fault, isn't it?'

'No, it's mine.' He got back into the front seat. 'I'm so besotted with that luscious body of yours that I couldn't give a damn about anything else. You might as well stay in the back, Megan. Try and get some sleep.'

'Sleep . . .? But I can't! I have to go home.'

'You're coming with me,' he said firmly.

'No, I—Please, Rome. I—Roddy wouldn't like it.'

'Roddy!' A white ring of anger appeared about his mouth. 'You're coming with me and no arguments. I'm not leaving you here with my dear little brother.'

Megan sat forward, her arms resting on the back of Jerome's seat, enabling her to see that the Jaguar was already eating up the miles to London. 'But what do I tell my family?' she asked desperately.

'Anything you want to.' He thrust the telephone receiver at her, getting her home number for her. 'Tell them my secretary walked out on me, that I need you to take notes at these meetings. Tell them anything, but you're coming with me.'

She didn't seem to be given a choice. His arrogance never ceased to amaze her, although this time she felt he had gone too far. 'There's a name for what you're doing,' she muttered. 'It's called kidnapping.'

'Don't worry, I'll make sure your terms of imprisonment aren't too uncomfortable,' he drawled mockingly.

Megan's face blazed, and then she heard Brian answer the telephone. 'Brian——'

'Megan!' His anger could be clearly heard. 'Where on earth are you?'

'I—er—I——' she gasped as Jerome took the telephone out of her hand.

'She's with me,' he told Brian. 'Yes, that's right. I

realise you and your mother must have been worried. It's all my fault, I didn't give Megan time to leave you a message. I need her in London. Yes, I have a dispute going on. Yes. Yes.' He put the receiver back down. 'Well, most of that was true,' he turned to say to Megan.

'It was?'

'Mm. I didn't give you time to leave a message. I do have a dispute going on. And I certainly need you. The fact that I need you in a completely different way from the one implied isn't important.'

'And how do you need me?' she asked shyly.

'In my bed,' he told her huskily. 'I don't know when I'll get away from this meeting, but when I do I want to know you're waiting for me.'

'Awaiting your pleasure?' Megan taunted bitterly.

'If you like to put it that way,' he nodded.

'I don't! You don't give a damn about anyone's wants or needs but your own, do you?' she accused heatedly. 'It isn't—convenient for me to go to London at the moment.' She dreaded to think what Roddy would do when he found out she had left with his brother.

'Your wants and needs concern me,' Jerome assured her. 'And right now you want and need me too.'

'I——'

'Don't lie to me, Megan,' he warned. 'I think I'm experienced enough to know a woman's reaction to me. Get some sleep, Megan, it's a long drive.'

'Surely you need to stop for a while,' she frowned. 'You can't make the return journey without at least having something to eat.'

His mouth was taut. 'If I stop at all it will be at a hotel, and it won't be to eat. I think we should just drive straight through.'

'Yes,' she agreed hastily. 'I don't suppose you would

consider dropping me off? I could still get home from here.'

'No. Roddy will survive without you,' he said grimly.

'But you don't understand——'

'I understand all right!' Jerome ground out. 'You have to choose, Megan, him or me.'

'Ch-choose?'

'Yes!' A fire burnt in his eyes, his expression was fierce. 'If I take you back to Roddy now he can damn well keep you. Well?'

Megan swallowed hard, torn both ways. If she went back she would be helping Patsy save her marriage, and yet if she did go back she would lose Jerome once and for all. But she had told Patsy she would help her. She couldn't just let her down——

'If it takes you this long to decide,' Jerome muttered angrily, 'Roddy can have you!' He slowed the car down and began to reverse it up a dirt-track.

'No!' she stopped him, clutching on to his arm. 'I— I'll come with you,' she told him breathlessly.

'Sure?'

'Yes,' she gave a vigorous nod.

His breath left his lungs in a loud hiss, his face pale in the moonlight. 'You realise you're saying yes to everything I want?'

She didn't care any more. She loved him. Maybe she was what he thought she was after all, because she knew that she had every intention of sleeping with him. She had to admit to being shocked by her own decision, but she felt no shame, only a quiet elation.

'Yes, I realise,' she smiled at him shyly.

'My God, Megan,' he gave a shaky sigh, 'don't ever do that to me again! I couldn't bear not to have you with me now.'

'I couldn't bear not to be with you,' she admitted

huskily. 'I think I will get some sleep after all,' she gave a contented smile. 'I think I may need it,' she added mischievously.

Jerome's throat chuckle was answer enough.

CHAPTER NINE

IT was after three when they arrived in London, and still dark, although there was some traffic on the streets even at this time of day. Jerome had called his assistant and managed to get the meeting arranged for four-thirty.

'Do you ever miss all this?' he turned to ask Megan.

'London, you mean?' She shrugged at his nod. 'Not really. I grew up here, but I never liked it much.'

He frowned. 'You'll be all right while I'm away all day?'

'Bored, probably,' she sighed. 'But no doubt I won't come to any harm. You have to leave right away?'

'More or less,' he confirmed. 'I'll take a shower, change my clothes, and then I'm afraid I'll have to leave you at the hotel.'

Colour flowed into her cheeks. 'I'll be staying there with you?'

He looked down at her with warm caressing eyes, Megan having moved back into the front of the car when they had stopped off halfway for petrol. 'Don't you want to?' he asked softly.

'Oh yes,' she made no effort to hide her feelings any more. 'I just thought——'

'I have a suite, darling,' Jerome gently touched her cheek. 'There's plenty of privacy. No one will disturb us, I'll make sure of that.'

She knew he would do just that, knew by the way he took command at the reception desk that he was highly respected here. The information that she was to share his suite didn't even raise an eyebrow.

It certainly was a suite—a large lounge, three bedrooms and three bathrooms. Megan walked from room to room in awe. A small vase of flowers alleviated the impersonality of the main bedroom, some discarded clothes were on the floor.

'Sorry about the mess,' Jerome said ruefully, pulling fresh clothes out of the wardrobe. 'I haven't had time to be tidy today.'

'That's all right.' She picked up a shirt from the floor, clutching it to her, at once aware of the tangy smell of his body clinging to the shirt.

Jerome watched her from the bathroom door, his gaze warm. 'Will you shower with me?'

'I—er—No, not now,' her cheeks were fiery red. 'There isn't really time,' she evaded. 'Maybe later.'

His eyes showed his disappointment. 'You're right, we don't want to rush it between us. I'll see you in a few minutes.' He gave a brief smile before closing the door.

Megan heard the hiss of the water as he turned on the shower. Would she be able to go through with this? Jerome seemed to assume she had done this sort of thing before. If only she were one of the liberated girls that dominated female society today! Instead she was a scared little girl, who knew nothing of a man's possession.

And what about Roddy? What would he do about her being here with Jerome?

Seconds later Jerome emerged from the bathroom, completely naked, donning his fresh clothes with unhurried ease. Megan watched him with fascination, unembarrassed because he wasn't. And with good reason—he was perfect, lean, muscular and beautiful.

He buttoned up his shirt, tucking it into his trousers. 'You're sure you'll be okay here while I'm out?'

'Yes, fine.' She seemed to have a permanent blush. 'I'll probably try and get some sleep.'

'God, yes.' He bent to kiss her briefly on the mouth. 'Megan . . .' he groaned. 'Oh God, Megan!'

She met him halfway, their bodies seeming to fuse together, Megan's arms up about his neck. 'Oh Rome, can't you stay here?' she pleaded.

His eyes darkened. 'I feel the same way, I'm impatient for you. But I have to go, darling, it's almost four-thirty now. I'll call you when I'm leaving.' He claimed her mouth in another soul-destroying kiss, finally, reluctantly leaving her.

Megan removed his discarded clothes from the bathroom, evidence of his worry about this stoppage. He was usually such a tidy person, his bedroom at The Towers hardly looked occupied, it was kept so scrupulously neat and tidy.

She took a shower herself, finally collapsing into the double bed, too weary to think of anything else but the fact that she would no doubt be sharing this bed with Rome in the very near future.

She was woken by a light knock on the outer door, hearing a key in the lock as she struggled through the blankets of sleep.

'Room Service,' a male voice called out. 'I've brought your breakfast, Miss Finch.'

Megan blinked dazedly, having been in a heavy sleep. 'Er—yes, yes,' she replied groggily. 'I—I won't be a moment.' She struggled out of bed, hastily pulling on Rome's white towelling robe.

A boy stood outside in the corridor, a laden tray in

his hands. 'Your breakfast, Miss Finch,' he repeated.

'Yes. Come this way,' she opened the door to the lounge. 'Please put it on the table.' She frowned her puzzlement. 'I didn't order this, you know.'

'No, Miss Finch,' he put the tray down on the dining-table that occupied one end of the room, 'Mr Towers ordered it for you.'

'Rom—er—Mr Towers did?' Her eyes were wide with surprise. 'When did he do that?'

'I'm not really sure, Miss Finch. Early this morning, I think. Before I came on duty anyway, and I was here at seven-thirty.'

So even with all his other worries Jerome had thought to provide her with food, probably realising she would be too embarrassed to order any herself. 'Thank you,' she smiled shyly at the boy.

He smiled back. 'If there's anything else you need, just call.'

Megan inspected the food once he had gone, finding scrambled eggs, grilled bacon and tomatoes, and plenty of toast, plus a pot of coffee. It was the sort of breakfast she wouldn't normally have eaten, but as it was almost lunchtime she found the meal very welcome.

After she had eaten she washed and dressed, finding her lack of clothes irksome. If she was going to stay here for any length of time she would have to get some new clothes.

The television in the lounge didn't provide much entertainment, so she walked down to the reception to buy a paperback.

'Megan!'

She turned to see Stella Mitchell, the other woman looking as beautiful as ever. 'Miss Mitchell,' she acknowledged awkwardly. 'Excuse me . . .' she turned to leave.

'Don't go,' Stella touched her arm. 'I'm here to see you.'

'Me?' Megan held the paperback she had just purchased defensively in front of her.

'Yes,' Stella smiled. 'Rome asked me to come.'

'Rome did?' She was aware of sounding like a parrot, but she couldn't help herself. Stella Mitchell's presence here was so unexpected.

'He thought you might be lonely,' Stella explained.

So he hadn't just provided food for her, he had provided company too. Much as Megan respected this woman she wished Rome had let her choose her own company, if she had wanted any. She would rather have just spent the day waiting for him.

Stella smiled as if reading her thoughts. 'He isn't sure when he'll be able to get away. Apparently the unions are getting tough, and Rome is determined not to give in. He told me to tell you to go out and enjoy yourself, that he could be there for days, snatching a couple of hours' sleep when he can.'

'Oh no!' Megan groaned. 'If he's going to be that long then I might as well go home.'

The other woman shook her head. 'I wouldn't advise it. Rome will only come after you again, and it doesn't seem to have done him much good the first time. The union leaders weren't very happy about his disappearance last night.'

'You mean it's my fault they're being difficult?'

Stella shrugged. 'Rome thinks it was worth it.'

'And you don't.'

'I didn't say that,' she smiled. 'Don't be so quick to take offence! I've never seen Rome like this about a woman before, you've got him in quite a state.'

'As you said, he likes to win,' Megan said ruefully.

Stella laughed. 'I'm glad you've stopped fighting him,

Megan. Right now he needs you very much.'

Megan blushed. 'Well, I'm here, aren't I?'

Stella squeezed her arm. 'Yes, you are, and I'm pleased that you are. Now, shall we go out to the shops? Rome told me it's some time since you last looked around London.'

Megan frowned. 'He seems to have spoken to everyone but me!'

'He presumed you would still be sleeping.'

Megan didn't miss the light reprimand in Stella's voice, and she smiled brightly. 'The shops, I think you said?'

It was late afternoon when they returned, having had tea out. There was no message for Megan from Rome, so she presumed he was still at his meeting. There were two other messages for her, though, one from Brian—and one from Roddy. She was undecided about which call she should return first. Brian's would probably be safest. He would probably be at home now too.

'Megan,' he sounded anxious, 'I've been waiting for your call all afternoon.'

'Sorry,' and she explained about having been out.

'But I thought you were helping Mr Towers?'

She blushed. 'I am. He—er—he didn't need me this afternoon.'

'Oh, I see. Well, I got the number of the hotel from Mrs Reece. There've been a couple of telephone calls for you here, both of them important. Although neither of them makes much sense to me,' he mumbled.

'Who were they from?' she asked sharply, suspecting Roddy of having been making mischief.

'One was from Tracy, that girl you were friendly with at the hospital. She said Miss Pryce, your Senior Nursing Officer, is reconsidering your dismissal.'

'She is?' Megan gasped.

'Mm. Tracy's told her something that made her wonder if she might have misjudged you. She said Miss Pryce was hoping to talk to the patient involved.'

Megan's heart sank. Roddy would never admit to anything. But Megan knew exactly what Tracy had told Miss Pryce—it had to be about her room number. 'Oh well,' she dismissed, 'we'll just have to wait and see, won't we? What was the other call?'

'This one makes even less sense. Patsy Jones called, she said to tell you that she's told Donald everything, and that it's going to be all right.'

Megan heaved a sigh of relief, her guilt about the other girl removed. 'Thank goodness for that!' Now Roddy had no hold over her.

'What did she mean?' Brian wanted to know.

'It's a long story, Brian.'

'One you aren't going to tell me, hmm?'

'Right,' she laughed.

'When are you coming home?'

'I—I'm not sure. As soon as this dispute is over, I suppose. I'll be needing some clothes, Brian——'

'That's all been taken care of,' he interrupted.

'It has?' Rome had been at work again. He seemed to think of everything.

'Yes,' Brian answered her. 'You had a visitor this morning too. You've suddenly become very popular,' he said suspiciously.

'Was it Paul?' she asked with reluctance.

'Paul? Don't be silly. He wouldn't need to visit, he works here.'

'Then who?'

'Roddy Meyers,' he informed her.

She gulped. 'R-Roddy?'

'Mm.'

'What did he want?' she asked with dread.

'He mentioned something about the two of you having a date for tonight. When I told him you were in London with his brother he offered to bring you some clothes.'

'You mean he's coming here?' she gasped.

'That's right. In fact, he should be there by now.'

So that was what his call had been about. 'Okay. Thanks, Brian,' she said dully. 'I'll—I'll be in touch.'

'Okay, love. Mum sends her love.'

'And I send mine.' Megan rang off abruptly.

Roddy was on his way here! Still, at least he no longer had that hold over her. Brave Patsy to have told Donald about Roddy.

She had no warning of Roddy's arrival; one minute she was sitting alone in the suite wondering what to do, the next he was in the room. She stood up slowly, eyeing him warily. 'What do you want?'

'Surprised to see me?' He ignored her question, putting her suitcase down on the floor at his feet, his expression unpleasant.

'Not at all,' she replied tautly.

'Ah, your brother let you know.'

'Yes.'

'What do you think you're doing here with Rome?' he rasped suddenly.

Megan blushed. 'What do *you* think I'm doing?'

'I warned you——'

'Patsy's told Donald everything,' she told him triumphantly.

'I see,' he said slowly. 'And you think that alters things between us?'

She looked disconcerted by his lack of surprise. 'Well, of course it does.'

'I don't agree.' His gaze ran over her insolently. 'We're alone here, aren't we?'

Megan began to feel nervous, not liking the look in his eyes. 'It's a hotel.'

He smiled, a smile without humour. 'But this is Rome's suite. No one will intrude in here unless specifically asked to do so.'

'You're here, and you weren't asked.'

'So I am,' he gave a husky laugh. 'And now I'm going to avail myself of the amenities.' He took a threatening step towards her.

'What do you mean?' Megan began backing away.

'I once told you that Rome would never be interested in a woman I've had first, and that still applies.'

'How do you know we haven't already——' She broke off as he twisted her arm painfully behind her back. 'Roddy, you're breaking my arm!' she cried.

'Have you been with Rome?' The tension on her arm didn't relax in the slightest degree.

'No!' She gritted her teeth.

He pulled her arm up even higher. 'Is that the truth?'

'Yes!' she told him faintly. 'Roddy, please . . .' Pain shot through her arm and everything suddenly went black.

She woke up to find herself lying on the bed, with Roddy bending over her as he kissed her, his hands roaming freely over her body. Nausea rose within her. 'Roddy——'

'You like this, don't you?' he bit her throat painfully. 'Tell me you like it, Megan.'

'Roddy——'

Suddenly he was pulled off her, landing against the far wall with a sickening thud. Jerome's anger filled the room, his eyes burning brown orbs in his pale face, his body tensed with furty.

Megan began to cry. 'Oh Rome, thank God you're here!' she choked, reaching out to him.

He ignored her outstretched hand, turning to look at his brother. 'Get up,' he ordered grimly.

Roddy rubbed the back of his head. 'So that you can knock me down again? No, thanks!'

'Get up!'

'She isn't worth it, Rome. Little sluts like her are two a——'

He didn't get any further as Jerome pulled him to his feet by a hand on the front of his shirt. His fist landed on Roddy's jaw with all the anger there was in him, knocking the younger man to the floor again. Roddy's expression was dazed.

'Get out of here!' Jerome turned away.

'Rome!' Megan cried out to him, her face white.

'As soon as my back was turned you got him here,' he accused fiercely. 'You were even making love with him on *my* bed!'

Making love? Surely Jerome couldn't think she had enjoyed that—that *disgusting* touch on her body?

'Rome, no!' she protested. 'He was forcing me, touching me against my will.'

'It looked like it,' he scorned savagely.

She looked at Roddy. 'Tell him,' she pleaded. 'Tell him I didn't want you here. Tell him, damn you!' she screamed shrilly.

Roddy slowly stood up. 'Forget it, Megan. You'll just have to settle for me.'

'Never!' she shuddered. 'You disgust me!'

'You aren't such a bargain yourself.' Jerome looked at her as if he couldn't bear the sight of her. He turned to his younger brother. 'You realise her reputation? According to rumour she was also dismissed from her last job for having men in her room.'

Megan's eyes widened. 'You heard about that?'

'Is it true?' he rasped.

She swallowed hard. 'I——'

'It's true,' Roddy cut in.

Jerome's eyes narrowed suspiciously. 'How do you know?'

Roddy shrugged. 'Ask Megan.'

'Well?' he demanded of her.

'I——' she licked her lips nervously. 'You see——'

'I was one of the men,' Roddy surprised her by admitting.

'*One* of the men?' Jerome asked raggedly.

'That's right.'

'Megan?'

She felt sick, the nausea was no longer going to be denied. She got up and ran to the bathroom, only just getting there in time. She was pale and weak by the time the nausea had passed, and the slamming of a door told her that one of the men had left. Oh, she hoped it was Roddy!

Roddy stood alone in the bedroom when she returned, a triumphant smile on his face. 'He's letting me have you,' he announced.

She swallowed hard. 'He said that?'

He grinned. 'He said worse, but it isn't repeatable.'

'Oh God!' She collapsed down on to the bed. 'Why do you have to destroy and hurt, Roddy? Why can't you let anyone be happy?'

'You think you could have been happy with Rome?' he scorned.

'I would have tried.'

'And in the end you would have had to admit defeat, as my father did with Rome's mother.'

'Your father?'

'My mother never loved him, you know.' He had retreated into some sort of private hell. 'My father loved her and all the time she still loved Rome's father.'

'But he was dead!'

'It didn't matter, she still loved him. My father was second best, and so was I. Rome always came first, always!' His hands clenched into fists at his side. 'That's the way the Towers family is, you see. They can love only once. Rome's too proud to fall in love with someone like you.' He turned to leave.

'Where are you going?' she asked sharply.

'Back to The Towers.' He grimaced. 'I don't think London is big enough for both Rome and me at the moment.'

'Can I come with you?' She was too weary to fight any more, knowing that she had lost Jerome for good.

His eyes widened. 'Are you sure you want to?'

She stood up, collecting her coat. 'Why not? I don't have anywhere else to go.'

She felt numb, not even noticing as Roddy's sports car ate up the miles between London and Norfolk.

'I've always admired Rome,' he said suddenly.

'You surprise me,' she taunted. 'I would have said you hated him.'

'No. I love him.'

'But you're jealous of him.'

'I suppose so,' he admitted. 'I have even more reason to feel jealous now, don't I?'

'Do you?' she said dully.

'You're in love with him.'

She turned to look at Roddy. 'And why should that make you jealous?'

'Would you believe, I love you myself?'

'No, I wouldn't believe!' She gave a choked laugh. 'No man in love would treat me as you have.'

'They might if they could see you weren't interested.'

Megan gave him a searching look, seeing his gaunt expression, the dejection in his bearing. 'Stop fabricating, Roddy,' she sighed. 'I'm too tired to play any more games. 'You've got your own way, there's no need to act this charade out any more.'

'It isn't a charade, Megan. If you could have loved me . . .' He drew a ragged breath, a white ring of tension about his mouth. 'I think I've been a little insane these last few weeks. It would seem I'm a Towers after all, and I've acquired all the family traits. I always thought I was on the outside, that I didn't belong. But I fell in love with you on sight, and you rejected me. It was another rejection in my life I couldn't take.'

Megan shook her head, unable to believe him. 'But you kept trying to force me,' she reminded him.

He sighed. 'I wanted you. I even followed you back to The Towers in the hope that I could still make you interested.'

'After getting me dismissed!' she scorned.

'I didn't mean it to go that far. I told your Nursing Officer that we were engaged, hoping to compromise you into marrying me, but you categorically denied any serious involvement between us. I didn't mean you to get thrown out, Megan, believe me.'

'And your involvement with Patsy?' He was so earnest that she was starting to believe he really meant all this.

'An effort on my part to make you jealous.'

'Couldn't you at least have chosen someone who wasn't already married?'

He shrugged. 'She was available.'

'Oh, Roddy!' Megan shook her head.

'I know—I've made a mess of things from start to finish. I'll take you back to Rome if you like.'

'What's the point?' Her expression was agonised. 'He doesn't want me, not now.'

'Are you kidding?' He gave a bitter laugh. 'I thought he was going to kill me just now.'

'You're lucky *I* didn't,' she told him ruefully. 'But it's no good, Roddy, Rome is no longer interested in me.'

'He will be once I've told him the truth.'

'You think I want him that way?' She shook her head. 'It's better like this. I think it's better if I admit defeat now, before I become too deeply involved.'

'Can you be any more involved than you are now?' Roddy asked gently.

'Oh yes, yes, I could!' Once she had given herself to Jerome there would be no turning back for her, she would have to remain in his life until he tired of her or found her replacement. 'In a way I'm grateful to you, Roddy. I was about to make a fool of myself. I—I'm sorry I can't love you. I never meant to hurt you.'

He sighed. 'And I never meant to hurt you either, I just couldn't seem to stop myself.'

The warmth of the car was making Megan fall asleep. She woke suddenly, sure that something was wrong, and opened her eyes just in time to see the lights of another car coming straight at them. She cried out as they didn't seem to deviate, knowing that the two vehicles were going to collide.

'Get down, Megan!' Roddy threw himself across her just as there was a tremendous crunch. The horrendous grinding of metal was the last thing she heard before she passed out.

CHAPTER TEN

THEY told her afterwards that Roddy had been killed on impact, that by protecting her he had risked and given his own life. Megan herself was in a state of shock for several days afterwards, but her cuts and bruises were superficial; only the knowledge that Roddy had given his life for her was scarring her internally.

The first person she saw when her eyes fluttered open as she lay between the crisp white sheets of the hospital bed was Jerome. He was sitting beside the bed holding her hand, very white, his eyes shadowed.

'I'm sorry,' her tongue seemed to be stuck to the roof of her mouth. 'About Roddy,' she added huskily.

'Yes.' His troubled gaze searched the pallor of her features. 'How do you feel?'

Tears gathered in her huge green eyes. 'How am I supposed to feel, knowing Roddy just died for me?' Her tone was bitter, and she removed her hand from beneath his.

'He did it because he wanted to,' Jerome said gently.

Tears trickled down her cheeks. 'He did it because he loved me. Oh God!' She turned her face into the pillow. 'Leave me. Please, leave me.'

'Megan——'

'Please go!'

She was allowed out of hospital a week later. Her visitors had been numerous, although she had seen no more of Jerome—at her request. His flowers had been turned away too, and after this rejection he didn't send any more.

164

Megan hadn't even been allowed out of hospital for Roddy's funeral, although her mother and Brian had attended. Her mother had told her afterwards that Jerome looked terrible, his face haggard, very gaunt. Megan hadn't wanted to hear how he looked; she didn't care any more.

Although completely recovered she was shrouded in a lethargy that refused to be shaken off; all the fight had gone out of her. Roddy had been obsessed with her, she knew that now, and that love had made him want to remove all that stood in the path of him getting her, not caring who or what he destroyed in the process. He had been sick—a love like that was like a disease. But this was no comfort to her; nothing could ease her guilt for not being able to love him.

'Will you see Paul, love?' Her mother came into the lounge, her expression anxious.

Megan knew her behaviour was worrying her family, and in the week since she had come out of hospital she had tried to be cheerful. That she had failed to fool them was obvious.

'Yes, I'll see him.' she gave a wan smile. 'You go off to your meeting at the Institute. I know there's one being held tonight.'

'I'm not going out and leaving you on your own.'

'But I'm not alone, Mum, Paul will be here to keep me company. Please go,' she pleaded. 'I'd like—you to.'

'Are you sure?' Still her mother hesitated.

'Very,' she nodded.

She hadn't been left alone for a moment since she came out of hospital, and she had begun to wonder if her family suspected she would do something desperate.

'Please, Mum,' she begged as her mother still hesitated.

'All right, then. But you make sure Paul stays with you until Brian or I get home.'

'Yes, Mum,' Megan smiled.

Paul came in a few minutes later; he was a regular visitor; their relationship was back on a friendly footing. 'Wendy sent you some magazines,' he put them down on the table. 'She'll be round tomorrow. She's out with Bill tonight.'

'Bill Pope?' Megan asked interestedly.

'Mm,' he nodded. 'They're thinking of getting engaged at Christmas. Bill's asked Dad if they can, anyway.'

'Oh, that's lovely. He's a nice boy.'

'She could have done worse,' he agreed grudgingly.

Megan smiled at his expression. 'I'm happy for them.'

'So am I.' He sighed. 'I just wish——'

'Please, Paul!' her voice was sharp.

'Sorry,' he bit his lip guiltily. 'Did you love him very much?'

She frowned. 'Roddy?'

'Well, of course Roddy.'

'But I—Who said I loved him?' she asked indignantly.

'Everyone. The way you've been acting, the way you've gone in on yourself,' he shrugged. 'It's obvious.'

Not to her! She was upset and sickened at Roddy's death, but she had been unable to love him. At the end she had been able to pity him, had been able to understand his sick obsession with her, but she still feared him. Not that she for one moment imagined the accident had been anything but that, but she had realised on that drive back that Roddy would never stop his pursuit of her, and that he would stop at nothing to get her.

'Are you going back to the hospital?' Paul

changed the subject.

'I have to go to the doctor for a final check-up, but——'

'I didn't mean that. Brian told me that you've had a letter from the hospital authorities clearing your name, that you can resume your studies as soon as you feel well enough to.'

'I'm not going back,' she said jerkily. 'I—I couldn't, not now.'

'But——'

'I'm not going back!' She had received the letter only that morning, and had ripped it up into tiny shreds. Her clearance had had nothing to do with Roddy's death, they stated that categorically, and yet somehow for her the stigma was still there. Tracy wanted to go back, but Megan didn't feel able to cope with that sort of work at the moment.

'Are you going back to work at The Towers, then?' Paul persisted.

'No!' She went pale. She couldn't even begin to think about seeing Jerome again, she hated him and his opinion of her. When he had walked out of that hotel room he had walked out of her life for good, had left her to Roddy. She didn't want anything to do with him now; she hadn't wanted his roses at the hospital, and wanted him even less. 'I'm not sure I still have a job there,' she added tightly.

Paul frowned. 'Has Mr Towers sacked you?'

'I don't think he can. We have a deal, you work for us and I work for him.'

'And as I'm still here that means you still have a job there.'

Megan's eyes narrowed suspiciously. 'Who put you up to this, Paul? Why this sudden interest in when I intend going back to work?'

Colour darkened his cheeks. 'I just thought——'

'Don't you mean Brian thought?' she cut in sharply. 'He's been asking me pretty much the same questions the last few days.'

'He's worried about you, we all are.'

'I can't think why.' She stood up, moving restlessly about the room, her figure almost wraithlike; her loss of weight over the last two weeks had been enormous. 'I'll be fine in a couple of weeks.'

'You can't mope about here for ever,' he insisted. 'You have to go out and face the world some time.'

'I've been out.'

'Down to the local shop,' he scorned. 'Wow!'

'I'm still feeling weak,' she defended.

'So you ought to, you don't eat enough to keep a bird alive.'

'I manage,' she said stiffly.

'Megan——'

'Please, Paul,' she put up a hand to her aching temple, 'I don't want to hear any more.'

He instantly looked concerned. 'Are you feeling ill?'

'Just a headache. But I think I should lie down. Would you mind . . .'

'No, of course not. I'm sorry, Megan, I was only doing it for the best.'

'I know,' she attempted a wan smile.

'Don't forget Wendy will be round tomorrow.' He kissed her lightly on the forehead.

Megan sat in the darkness once he had left, staring sightlessly at the fire, but its warmth did not reach her. Why didn't they just leave her alone? She didn't want to go back to work at the hospital, and she wanted to go back to The Towers even less. Jerome was there. Jerome, the man she still loved, despite his cruel rejection of her. He hadn't given her a chance to defend herself, had condemned her out of hand.

Again she stood up, the restlessness a part of her now, a need to escape to—heaven knew what! She didn't give herself any more time to think, but grabbed up her coat and ran out into the night. In the darkness that protected her she didn't have to question her actions, didn't have to probe the deep wound Jerome had left in her heart.

'Megan . . .'

At the first sound of that husky voice she thought it was an extension of her tortuous thoughts, thought that Jerome had appeared before her at will. Then she felt the labrador jumping up her, barking joyously as she licked Megan's face.

'Honey!' that voice rapped out authoritatively. 'Heel, girl!'

The dog instantly left Megan to run back to her master, her tail wagging excitedly. Megan's face paled as she saw Jerome standing a few feet away from her. He was dressed in dark clothing, his face appearing ghostly in the gloom. With a startled cry Megan turned on her heel and walked away.

Strong fingers stopped her, and Jerome's grasp tightened about her arm as she struggled to be free. 'Be still, Megan,' he ordered gruffly.

She obeyed, looking up at him with chilling eyes. 'Let go of me,' she requested coldly.

'You won't run?' His brown gaze avidly searched her features.

'No,' she agreed huskily.

He instantly set her free, his gaze intent on her averted face. 'How are you?' he asked finally.

Her mouth twisted bitterly. 'How do I look?'

'Terrible,' he admitted ruefully.

'So do you.' She had been aware of that much at

least. His face was finely drawn, deep lines beside his nose and mouth, his eyes bleak. 'I'm sorry I wasn't able to go to Roddy's f-funeral,' she faltered. 'I—The doctor wouldn't let me go.'

'I understood. Megan——'

'I think I should go now,' she interrupted jerkily, still unable to look at him. 'They don't know I'm out at home, and they'll worry.'

'When are you coming back, Megan?'

Now she did look at him, her heart contracting at the sorrow etched into every feature of his strong face. 'Back where?' she asked breathlessly, unable to look away now that she had once gazed at him.

'To The Towers. I've had several telephone calls that only you can deal with, calls about the Christmas party.'

Her eyes widened. 'You're still going ahead with that?'

He sighed. 'Children don't understand things like death.'

'No, I suppose not,' she agreed dully. 'I—I'm not coming back.'

'Memories?' Jerome asked sharply.

'You could say that.' And the need to keep as far away from him as possible!

'They have to be faced, Megan.'

'No, they don't.'

'Coward!' he rasped.

She blinked dazedly. 'I—You—What did you say?'

'Nothing goes away just because you choose to ignore it.'

'I know that!' The pain of loving him hadn't gone away, no matter how she had ridiculed or denied it.

'Then come back, face it all.'

'I can't! The hospital have offered me my job back,'

she told him in a rush.

Jerome's eyes narrowed. 'Why?'

'Because they've decided I wasn't in the wrong after all. Rod—The man in my room wasn't there by invitation.'

His hand grasped her arm once again. 'You said Roddy,' he reminded her hardly. 'Was he the man?'

'I——'

'Was he?' Jerome shook her.

'You already know he was in my room, he told you so himself,' she snapped.

'He was the only man?'

'Yes!'

'I should have known,' he muttered grimly.

'You don't understand. Roddy—He was in love with me.'

'I know,' Jerome nodded.

Megan's look sharpened. 'How do you know?'

'He told me, that last evening.'

'I see,' she bit her lip. 'He didn't mean to get me dismissed,' it was suddenly imperative that she clear Roddy of all blame. 'It just went wrong.'

'Yes, very wrong. So when can I expect you back at The Towers?' he asked briskly.

'I told you, I——'

'We have a bargain, Megan,' he said harshly. 'And I've kept to my side of it. Are you saying you want to back out?'

There was a steely determination about him that warned her he would not let her go as easily as that. 'I—I'm still signed off work,' she excused.

He nodded tersely. 'When you get the okay to come back you know the way.' He turned and walked away, a lone man followed obediently by the golden labrador.

It was another two weeks before the doctor decided she was well enough to go back to work, and it had taken her that long to gain the courage to walk up the long drive of The Towers.

There were only three weeks left to Christmas now, two weeks to the actual party, and it would take her all that time to complete the arrangements.

'Oh, it's so good to see you, love,' Freda greeted her warmly. 'Go over to the fire and warm yourself. I'll make us a coffee, shall I?'

It was exactly the balm she needed to her mood, the weather as bleak as she felt. Freda asked no pointed questions and after two cups of coffee Megan began to feel more normal, less the object of pity she had been since she had been discharged from the hospital.

The telephone was ringing when she walked into the study, where Jerome was intent on some papers in front of him. 'Answer that, will you?' He didn't even look up.

It was a call about the supply of paper hats for the party, and she dealt with it quickly and efficiently, arranging for their delivery. When she put the telephone down it was to find Jerome looking at her in disbelief.

'You're here,' he said breathlessly.

Megan held her head proudly erect. 'You told me I had to be.'

'I expected you to let me know *when* you were coming back.' He regained some of his composure, his eyes narrowed. 'Not just walk in.'

'I did try to get in touch with you over the weekend, but Mrs Reece said you were in London.'

'I see,' he said tightly.

'If it isn't convenient . . .'

'Oh, it's convenient,' he gave a harsh laugh. 'The

estate correspondence is days behind. With your help I should be able to deal with most of that today.'

Megan was exhausted by the end of the morning, the huge volume of work had come as a great shock after her inactivity of the last few weeks.

'Have lunch with me,' Jerome said as she moved to the door.

She didn't even turn. 'No, thank you.'

Her mother was waiting for her in the kitchen. 'All right?' she asked anxiously.

'Fine.' Megan forced a bright smile to her lips. 'The arrangements for the party are going very well.' She chattered all the way home, putting her mother's mind completely at rest.

When she returned to The Towers after lunch it was to find Jerome in the kitchen, the faithful Honey at his heels. She knew he watched her as she hung up her coat, felt his eyes on the slenderness of her body, on the gauntness of her face.

'Would you help me in the study again this afternoon?' he asked her. 'We could get rid of most of the backlog that way.'

Megan shrugged. 'I have no objection.' After all, it was his deal.

His mouth tightened. 'Good,' he said tautly, picking up the tray of coffee from the table and walking through to the study. 'Would you do the honours?' He seated himself behind the desk, still watching her.

She poured out his coffee as she knew he liked it, handing it to him silently. She sat down at her own desk, her hands in her lap as she waited for him to begin work.

'Aren't you having one?' he indicated the second cup on the tray.

'No, thank you,' she replied primly.

His cup landed in the saucer with a clatter. 'We have to talk, Megan.' He stood up and came round to the front of the desk. 'Surely you can see that?'

Megan eyed him coldly. 'We have nothing to talk about.' She picked up her notepad. 'Now, could we get on with these letters?'

'No, we damn well can't!' He took the notepad out of her hands and threw it down on the desk, pulling her to her feet. 'Megan!' he groaned, pulling her roughly against him. 'Oh, Megan, love me. For God's sake love me,' he moaned, his face buried in her throat as his body shook against her.

She had gone white, and now grey, rigid in his arms. 'Take your hands off me!' she told him hysterically.

'I can't!' He rained fevered kisses over her face, breathing heavily, his arms like steel bands about her. 'I need you, Megan. Don't be cold towards me, darling. I can't stand it.'

'And I can't stand your hands on me!' she said disgustedly. 'I'm not interested, Jerome, not any more.'

Now he was white too, lines of strain beside his nose and mouth. 'Megan——'

'Let go of me,' she ordered through gritted teeth. 'Your touch disgusts me!'

At once his hands fell away from her. 'You can't mean that,' he choked.

'I can,' she said coldly. 'Your brother has been dead a month, and already you're after me again. I'm leaving now, Mr Towers, and I won't be coming back. You can please yourself what you do about the deal you have with Brian, I don't care about it any more. I'll explain to Brian that it was my fault.'

Jerome turned away. 'That won't be necessary. The deal stands.'

'Why should it?'

'It stands,' he said rigidly.

'All right,' she shrugged. 'But I meant it about not coming back.'

'I know. I'll okay things with Brian. And I won't come near you again.'

'That's all I ask,' she told him quietly.

She was alone at home when Brian came in, serving up his meal for him. 'Mum's just popped out to the shop,' she told him.

'What are you doing at home?' He tucked hungrily into his meal.

'Hasn't Mr Towers spoken to you?' she frowned.

Brian watched her closely. 'He has. But I wanted to hear your side of it.'

'He made a pass at me and I walked out,' she said dully.

'Megan!' he reprimanded.

'Don't you believe me?'

'Quite frankly, no. I don't think it can be called making a pass when both parties are attracted to each other,' he told her bluntly.

'I'm not——'

'Don't, Megan,' he said gently. 'I may not be super-intelligent, but I'm not stupid either. I know that when you went to London you went solely to be with Jerome Towers.'

'He told you that?' she gasped.

'No, of course he didn't—I guessed. But you're old enough to make your own decisions about these things.' He shrugged. 'Obviously it went wrong and you argued, and that's the reason you were with Roddy when the accident happened. But whatever the argument was about Mr Towers seems to want to forget all about it. Why can't you do the same?'

'You wouldn't understand,' Megan choked.

'Try me.'

'I—I couldn't. I'm sorry, Brian.' She ran out of the room and up to her bedroom.

This was the first time she had cried since she had told Jerome to leave her alone after the accident. Up until now her feelings seemed to be locked inside her, her pain was too acute to be allowed release.

Roddy had died for her, and given his life to save her. He had loved her, she loved Jerome, and Jerome loved—no one. It was all such a waste.

What was to become of them all she didn't know. The whole of her family were at the mercy of Jerome, and after the way she had rebuffed him today she didn't think he would be in the mood to be charitable.

She was wrong. Jerome had proved himself to be the fair man everyone said he was, had kept his promise to make Brian his estate manager, and Brian was even now working alongside Jeff learning the job.

They had all sat down and discussed the situation logically. Brian had accepted that with two men working the land it just about paid for itself, but he had also accepted that without Jerome's help there wouldn't be two men, they certainly couldn't ever afford to pay one themselves.

So Brian had gone to Jerome and offered him the land. Megan found it all a relief in the end, and she knew her mother was glad it was over. Her mother was away for a few days at the moment, had gone to stay with her sister and ask her advice on Brian and Joyce's wedding. Megan felt sorry for the young couple; all the arrangements seemed to have been taken out of their hands.

Megan had seen nothing of Jerome, as he had promised she wouldn't, although Brian often spoke about him. Brian told her that the dispute at Jerome's factory had finally been settled amicably, although it had been delayed somewhat by Jerome's bereavement.

Megan now helped out at the local kindergarten, although she received no wages. It gave her something to do, and she found the children's naturalness very refreshing.

One poor little soul was still left waiting for his mother this morning, and Megan watched as he waited impatiently for his mother to arrive.

Finally Davy's bottom lip began to tremble. 'I'm going to miss the party,' he choked, looking up at her with tears in his eyes.

Megan put her arm around his shoulders. 'I'm sure she'll be here soon,' she comforted.

'But I'll miss the party!'

'What party, Davy?'

'The Christmas party.' Tears started to fall in earnest. 'I'll miss Father Christmas!' he wailed.

Megan bit her lip, having expected it to be a birthday party of something like that. 'You were going up to The Towers?'

'Yes,' he hiccupped. 'Mummy was taking me. She——' he broke off as the telephone began to ring. 'I bet that's my mummy!'

It was indeed his mummy. There had been a minor crisis with the baby of the house, and she pleaded with Megan to take Davy up to the party for her.

One look at Davy's tear-stained face was enough to tell her she couldn't refuse. 'Very well, Mrs Cooper,' she agreed rigidly. 'But you'll have to make sure Davy is picked up from there, I won't be staying.' The young mother assured her Davy would be collected, so Megan was left with one little boy eager to join in the festivities and meet Father Christmas.

She didn't have time to think of the fact that she hadn't been near The Towers in the four weeks since she had walked out of its doors, didn't have time to think of the fact that she might accidentally catch a glimpse of Jerome.

Davy hopped and skipped all the way, his smile one of complete happiness. How nice to be this young, to have an innocence to the harsh blows life could unexpectedly deal you.

Megan could hear the noise as soon as she reached the door. The house sounded as if it had been taken over by a group of shrieking banshees. No one came to answer her knock, so she let herself in, and the reason no one had come to the door soon became obvious. The whole place was in uproar, Mrs Reece and the rest of the staff failing to get any sort of order. There were children everywhere, and Megan feared for some of Jerome's china pieces, although he didn't seem to be in evidence to protect them. He was probably in London, well away from all this, and Megan couldn't blame him; chaos reigned here.

It was left to her to try and bring some order to the proceedings. 'How about a game?' she shouted above the noise.

A few of the children stopped to listen. 'What sort of game?' one of them asked.

'How about—Pass the Parcel?' She looked at them hopefully. They seemed undecided. 'I want you all in the lounge,' she told them in a brisk voice. 'All of you!' she said firmly.

Surprisingly they did as they were told, and she soon had a box of chocolates with layer upon layer of wrap-

ping to be passed from child to child. One of the older
children volunteered to play the piano, so Megan left
them to it.

'Thank goodness you've arrived!' Mrs. Reece gave a
weary sigh. 'I think they've all turned into little demons
since last year. Mr Towers would insist on giving them
the run of the house.'

Megan frowned. 'Even the old Squire didn't go that
far. Everywhere looks lovely, anyway.' The rooms were
decorated with balloons and paper-chains, a huge
decorated tree stood in one corner of the lounge, the
little fairy lights twinkling warmly. The food had all
been laid out on a trestle table, just waiting for the little
monsters to devour it.

She arranged a couple more games, but finally she
could tell the children were getting restless. 'What do
we do now?' she whispered to Mrs Reece, quite for-
getting she had wanted to leave after delivering
Davy.

'Mr Towers should be coming in any moment, he
was delayed in London,' the housekeeper whispered
back.

'You mean he's here?' Megan squeaked.

'Of course. Here he comes now,' Mrs Reece sighed
her relief.

Megan felt sure that the housekeeper knew what she
was talking about, and that Jerome really was inside
that Father Christmas costume somewhere, but it was
hard to tell under all that padding. He had certainly
dressed the part, despite his earlier reluctance, and the
heavy sack on his back attracted a great deal of attention.

She felt a lump gather in her throat as the children
crowded around him, ducking behind a tree as he
seemed to search the room. Each child went up to re-

ceive a gift, all of them with the child's name on, each stopping to whisper in 'Santa's' ear what they would like from him on Christmas Day.

Jerome was marvellous at it, Megan had to admit. There was a gentleness about him she had never seen before.

'Megan's turn, Megan's turn!' the children began to chant.

She swallowed hard, feeling strong young hands pulling her forward. Jerome looked at her with a start of surprise as the children abandoned her before him.

Were Santas supposed to have that sensual warmth in their eyes? She didn't think so.

'Would you like to sit on my knee and tell me what you'd like for Christmas?' he invited softly.

She blushed. 'I don't think so,' she shook her head.

'But you must.' He pulled her down on to his knee, the children giggling at them. Jerome's hand rested just below her breast, his eyes even warmer this close to. 'What would you like, Megan?' he prompted.

She was breathing hard, her heart suddenly melting. 'You,' she revealed achingly.

She could feel him tense. 'Me?' he repeated tautly.

'Yes,' she confirmed longingly.

'You want me in your stocking on Christmas morning?' he persisted uncertainly.

Megan was mesmerised by the fire burning in his eyes. 'I had somewhere a bit more comfortable in mind,' she murmured throatily.

'Then you've got me.' He stood up, pushing her off his lap. 'Serve the food, Mrs Reece,' he said softly. 'Megan and I will be upstairs if it all gets too much for you.'

Megan allowed herself to be dragged up the stairs,

wondering if she had gone completely insane. As soon as she had seen him again the past hadn't seemed to matter; his sensitivity and love towards the children showed her what a truly kind man he was.

'Wait here while I get these things off.' He pushed her forcibly down on his bed before going into the adjoining bathroom.

All Megan's uncertainty returned once she was alone. What was she doing here? Nothing had changed, nothing ever could change the fact that Jerome merely wanted to sleep with her. She stood up, hurrying to the door.

'Oh no, you don't!' Jerome swung her round, pulling her against the muscled tautness of his body, his only clothing a blue towelling robe. 'You aren't going anywhere,' he told her huskily.

'I must.' She daren't look at him. 'It was a mistake, all a mistake.'

'The only mistake is that I should have done this sooner.' His dark head swooped and he claimed her mouth in the sweetest, most drugging kiss they had ever shared. 'Megan . . .' he probed her lips apart. 'Megan, I love you,' he groaned.

She stiffened. 'Love . . .?'

'What's the matter?' His eyes darkened with pain. 'Don't you believe me?'

She frowned at the gauntness of him, at the air of weary defeat that seemed to surround him. 'Rome——'

He sighed. 'You don't believe me. I do love you, Megan, I've always loved you. Why do you think every man who came near you suddenly became a threat? Why do you think I reacted so violently to finding Roddy at the hotel with you? Believe me, I don't usually fight over women.'

'Is that why you left me with him, because you love

me?' she scorned bitterly.

'I didn't leave you with him, *you* left with him.'

'You told me to go,' she accused.

'I told Roddy to go,' he corrected. 'When I got back to the suite you'd gone too. Why did you go to London with me if you loved Roddy?' he sounded agonised.

'I didn't love him. At the end I felt sorry for him, but I never loved him.'

'At the hospital——'

'There's no point in bringing up the past, it isn't going to help matters. Roddy had the mistaken idea that I had a secret passion for him. I didn't.'

'You didn't love him?'

'No.'

'You don't love him now?'

'Not you too! No, I don't love him. But I'm sorry he died. It was my fault—he was trying to save me.'

'Thank God he succeeded!' Jerome shuddered. 'If you'd died I would have wanted to die too.'

'Rome . . .' she gasped in disbelief.

'I would. But I can't understand this—you and Roddy were always whispering together about something.'

'Well, it certainly wasn't the fact that we loved each other.' Megan looked away.

He frowned. 'You once told me there was someone else in his life, someone he didn't want me to know about. I—My God, Patsy Jones! It was her, wasn't it? That was why you suddenly seemed very involved with the Jones family.'

'It was just spite on Roddy's part,' she hastened to excuse. 'He thought it would make me jealous. His love for me was—obsessive.' She still shuddered when she thought of it.

'Like his father's for my mother,' Jerome said quietly. 'He was like that about her. It finally got to the stage where she couldn't stand it any more, and she left him. Frank committed suicide.'

'Oh, my God!' she groaned.

'Yes,' Jerome sighed. 'My mother never got over it. But you will,' he said fiercely. 'I'll make sure of that.'

'Roddy didn't crash on purpose,' she insisted. 'It was an accident.'

'And I went through hell because of it,' he moaned. 'I seem to have been going through one kind of hell or another ever since I first met you. I've been terrified, suspicious, of every man who comes near you. I reached the point of no return with you a long time ago, both physically and mentally.'

'But you left me to Roddy.' She couldn't hold back her bitterness. 'Roddy hurt me so much that day, twisting my arm behind my back, that in the end I fainted. He was furious because I'd gone to London with you. He came to the hotel with the intention of making love to me. I was just regaining consciousness after my faint when you burst in on us. You—you made vile accusations,' she remembered shakily.

'But I didn't mean for you to go! I came after you, you know.'

Her eyes widened with disbelief. 'You did?'

'How do you think I got to the hospital so quickly? I wasn't far behind you. When I saw the crumpled wreck of Roddy's car, and the police told me someone had been killed, I nearly went insane. When I reached the hospital and they told me you were still alive I just sat down and cried. Then when you woke up you told me to leave, would have nothing more to do with me.'

Megan swallowed hard. 'I thought——'

'You thought I still wanted to have an affair with you. You still think that.'

'And do you?' she challenged.

'A lifelong one,' he admitted huskily. 'One that will take us even beyond life.'

'Are you asking me to marry you?' she asked breathlessly.

'I'm begging you to.' Jerome avidly searched her features for some response to his proposal. 'I'm asking you to try and love me,' he added pleadingly.

'Even though you believe I've taken other lovers?'

'Yes.'

'Don't you mind about these other lovers?'

'I hate them like hell!' Jerome told her savagely. 'I didn't realise how possessive I was until I fell in love with you. It hasn't been an easy lesson. Megan, a little while ago you told me you wanted me—well, you've got me, for a lifetime. Would you—could you ever come to love me?'

Megan didn't like to see this arrogant man bowed by his love for her, hated to see his humility. 'The day we met, you changed your mind about asking me out. Why?'

'I thought you might feel embarrassed, working at The Towers, and dating me. Believe me, as soon as your mother was well enough to return I would have asked you out. Then you showed me in no uncertain terms that you didn't like me, so I came up with the idea of a deal with Brian as a means of keeping you at The Towers.'

She smiled, her last uncertainty removed. 'My mother once told me that The Towers needed a couple of children running about in it to make it into a home. But I don't think she thought they would be her grandchildren.'

A fierce light entered the darkness of his eyes. 'Do you love me?' he asked disbelievingly.

'Insanely,' she laughed. 'But I'm going to need some

convincing about your loving me.'

'Oh, I'll convince you,' he promised throatily, taking a threatening step towards her.

She licked her lips nervously. 'There's something else I think you should know.' She took a deep breath. 'Something you have to know before we're married.'

Jerome seemed to pale. 'What is it?'

'You may not like it.'

'*What is it?*'

'I'm not experienced, Rome. I've never had a lover, not one, and I'm not sure I'll even know how to start.'

He looked long and deeply into her completely innocent eyes, finally pulling her gently against him. 'How I've misjudged you,' he groaned. 'What an idiot I've been!'

'You don't mind?' she frowned up at him.

'Mind? I'm bloody ecstatic! Oh, Megan!' He picked her up and swung her round. 'Hey, I've just thought of the perfect wedding gift from your mother. Bertha,' he revealed smilingly. 'She brought *us* together, it's only fair that she should be back with the herd she misses so much.'

Megan glowed up at him. 'I think that's a wonderful idea. Mum's going to live with Aunt Rose once Brian is married, and there's really no room for Bertha at the farm now. Now I think we should go back downstairs, it is your party.'

He suddenly became serious. 'I much prefer my own private party up here. Besides, if we start now maybe our own child could attend next year.'

'Rome!' she pretended shock, but was secretly thrilled at his mastery.

'Mm?' He bent to caress her earlobe.

'I—Oh nothing.' She gave herself up to the man she

loved, knowing that their future would take care of itself. Right now the present was enough— more than enough.

Harlequin Plus

COOKING WITH HERBS

The key to turning a plain dish into memorable cuisine is the effective use of herbs. Not only do herbs add flavor and provide that extra hint of aroma or coloring, they are also rich in vitamins and aid digestion.

Following is a list of the more popular herbs and the foods they best enhance. Remember that the object is not to overwhelm natural flavors, so a pinch is often all you need.

HERBS	FOODS
anise	sweet rolls, breads, fruit pies, shellfish
basil	sauces, salads, tomatoes, seafood, eggs
bay	stews, stuffings, sauces, meat, seafood, poultry
caraway	borscht, cabbage soup, breads, cookies, dips, cheese spreads
coriander	pea and chicken soups, pastries, dressings, Spanish dishes
dill	dips, dressings, potato salad, chowders, cottage cheese
garlic	meats, sauces, stews, Italian, Spanish and Greek dishes
mustard	salads, dressings, sauces, fish, soups, spreads, eggs
oregano	green salads, omelets, Italian and Mexican dishes
rosemary	stuffings, marinades, sauces, green salads, poultry
sage	pork, lamb stuffings, fish chowders, consommés
tarragon	seafood, chowders, chicken soup, sauces, salads, marinades, veal, poultry, eggs
thyme	brown sauces, pickled beets, fricassees, meat, poultry, creole and gumbo dishes

Readers all over the country say Harlequin is the best!

"You're #1."

A.H.*, Hattiesburg, Missouri

"Harlequin is the best in romantic reading."

K.G., Philadelphia, Pennsylvania

"I find Harlequins are the only stories on the market that give me a satisfying romance, with sufficient depth without being maudlin."

C.S., Bangor, Maine

"Keep them coming! They are still the best books."

R.W., Jersey City, New Jersey

*Names available on request.

Harlequin Presents...

Take these 4 best-selling novels FREE

That's right! FOUR first-rate Harlequin romance novels by four world renowned authors, FREE, as your introduction to the Harlequin Presents Subscription Plan. Be swept along by these FOUR exciting, poignant and sophisticated novels . . . . Travel to the Mediterranean island of Cyprus in **Anne Hampson**'s "Gates of Steel" . . . to Portugal for **Anne Mather**'s "Sweet Revenge" . . . to France and **Violet Winspear**'s "Devil in a Silver Room" . . . and the sprawling state of Texas for **Janet Dailey**'s "No Quarter Asked."

Join the millions of avid Harlequin readers all over the world who delight in the magic of a really exciting novel. SIX great NEW titles published EACH MONTH! Each month you will get to know exciting, interesting, true-to-life people . . . . You'll be swept to distant lands you've dreamed of visiting . . . . Intrigue, adventure, romance, and the destiny of many lives will thrill you through each Harlequin Presents novel.

 **The very finest in romantic fiction**

Get all the latest books before they're sold out!

As a Harlequin subscriber you actually receive your personal copies of the latest Presents novels immediately after they come off the press, so you're sure of getting all 6 each month.

Cancel your subscription whenever you wish!

You don't have to buy any minimum number of books. Whenever you decide to stop your subscription just let us know and we'll cancel all further shipments.

Your FREE gift includes

Sweet Revenge by **Anne Mather**
Devil in a Silver Room by **Violet Winspear**
Gates of Steel by **Anne Hampson**
No Quarter Asked by **Janet Dailey**

FREE Gift Certificate
and subscription reservation
Mail this coupon today!

In the U.S.A.
1440 South Priest Drive
Tempe, AZ 85281

In Canada
649 Ontario Street
Stratford, Ontario N5A 6W2

Harlequin Reader Service:

Please send me my 4 Harlequin Presents books free. Also, reserve a subscription to the 6 new Harlequin Presents novels published each month. Each month I will receive 6 new Presents novels at the low price of $1.75 each [*Total – $10.50 a month*]. There are no shipping and handling or any other hidden charges. I am free to cancel at any time, but even if I do, these first 4 books are still mine to keep absolutely FREE without any obligation.

NAME   (PLEASE PRINT)

ADDRESS

CITY   STATE / PROV.   ZIP / POSTAL CODE

Offer expires July 31, 1982   SB479
Offer not valid to present subscribers

Prices subject to change without notice.